George wasted no time. He threw his weight against the door, heard a cracking noise, and saw that the wood of the frame had started to crack around the chain bracket. Before the man inside could close the door, George barged against it once more: the wood splintered, and the door banged open. The man in the room was thrown backwards by this, and as George stumbled through he almost tripped over the man's prostrate body. He tried to scramble away from George, then changed his mind and lunged at him, trying to catch his legs and bring him to the ground.

With a practised movement George booted the man in his stomach, hard enough to hurt, but not enough to injure. George was released, and he scrambled on into the main room. He saw Simone at once.

She was on the bed, naked and bound . . .

Mona Lisa

JOHN LUTHER NOVAK

**A novelisation based on the screenplay
by Neil Jordan and David Leland**

SPHERE BOOKS LIMITED

First published in Great Britain by
Sphere Books Ltd 1986
27 Wright's Lane, London W8 5SW
Copyright © 1986 by Sphere Books Ltd
Novelisation by John Luther Novak
Based on the screenplay by Neil Jordan

**TRADE
MARK**

Set in 10/13 pt Compugraphic Times

Printed and bound in Great Britain by
Cox & Wyman Ltd, Reading

Chapter 1

The other cons had told him it was the air you noticed when you were out. Air doesn't always have to smell of shit, they said. You think this normal . . . wait until you smell real air again. George hadn't listened, his mind somewhere away on another matter, but now he was out he remembered.

They were wrong, though. Air that stank of shit-buckets had never smelt normal to him, and the memory of it had left him as quickly as the contents of the same buckets usually vanished down the drain in the mornings. Dozing on the overnight train from Durham, uncomfortable in his clothes, George had been thinking about the noises. Nicks were bloody noisy places, night and day: doors crashing open and closed, the mesh in the stairwell clattering when any-one moved along the galleries, people shouting all the time, kicking up a racket because everyone there, screws and prisoners alike, were bored out of what-ever passed for brains. The train had seemed almost silent to him: twice he had wiggled his finger in his earhole, disbelieving. Maybe they'd made trains better in the last seven years, but that didn't seem likely. The sandwiches were still the same.

Now he stood in the road outside King's Cross, relishing the peace and quiet of early-morning

London. It was still too soon for commuters: lorries were grinding past, heading to or from the markets, a few cars and taxis scattered amongst them. They made a lovely noise: engines, tyres, exhausts . . . peace and quiet, London style.

Over to one side, near where the steps led down to the Underground, a young woman in a grimy apron was opening up a flower stall. She and the driver of a small truck were unloading flowers, standing them in plastic buckets in unplanned rows.

George watched for a while, his fingers exploring the unaccustomed tightness of his waistband. He had always been a great dresser: this was the suit he had been wearing when they sent him down. That was what prison was all about. They take seven years out of your life, and just so's you won't notice, at the end of it all they turf you out in the clothes you had gone in wearing, thinking you wouldn't mind. Maybe you wouldn't, but it makes you *notice* what all that time sitting around does to your gut. Trying to sleep on the train, folding himself uneasily in the vertical seat, George had loosened the top of his trousers and zipper until he realised it made him look like a slob. He'd never been a slob, not even when he was a kid.

He needed some new clothes, and he needed some exercise. Maybe not even in that order.

He walked over to the flower stand as the truck drove away. The girl was now unloading flowers from the buckets into wooden boxes lined with green stuff supposed to look like fronds.

She noticed him standing there, but ignored him.

'You got any daffodils?' George said.

'Over there.'

2

They were at the far end of the stall, high up at the back. George reached over and took down a bunch. They were still wet, and bound tightly together with elastic bands.

'Seventy pence,' the girl said.

He had started reaching for his pocket before it sunk in.

'Seventy pence for a pathetic little bunch like this?'

She shrugged. George fingered through the coins: some of them were his, seven years old, some of them were the remains of the rehabilitation hand-out. He passed over the money.

'You going to wrap them, then?' he said.

'Ask me nicely.'

'I just did.'

But she already had the paper in her hand, took the flowers from George and swirled them expertly into a neat cone, tweaking the pointed end into double thickness to make a grip. The water didn't seem to seep through with the paper folded like that.

'Thanks,' George said, but the girl had already abandoned him. She was back with the flowers, liberating them from their buckets.

He walked across London, saving money but thinking of the exercise as a way of getting his weight down. Not that he looked or felt overweight, but the reunion with his old clothes had come as a mild shock. George had always held his weight well: it distributed evenly over a strong frame, and he had never cut down on anything, had never tried. It was just the way he always used to live: a lot of getting about, a lot of *doing* things . . . sitting on the edge of a narrow bed

3

for most of a day wasn't natural to him.

London looked good, but then it would. A few new buildings, but a lot of the old ones. As the rush hour built up, the sheer amount of traffic surprised him. Some of the cars had their number plates lettered the wrong way round: A and B and C at the front . . . no one had told him that that had changed. And there were a lot of foreign cars, or more than he remembered. None of it mattered, except that he needed a car for himself and he had no idea of how he would get one.

Still, cars were never a problem, when you knew how.

He crossed Battersea Bridge, pausing in the centre to look down at the water, then along the river in both directions. He had never felt romantic about London – it was just the place he had always lived in – but it was good to be back. He did, after all, like the smell.

On the south side of the river he saw a newsagent's shop, and went in. He counted his money surreptitiously, then bought a box of chocolates, choosing the one with the biggest box that cost the least. He asked the woman behind the counter to wrap it up for him, make it look good, but she wouldn't put fancy paper around it. She offered to sell him some – twenty-six bleeding pence – but George settled for a brown paper bag.

He went on, enjoying the growing familiarity of the streets he was passing through.

Small groups of kids, most of them black, were wandering off to school. Some of them stared at him, and he stared back.

At last he turned the corner into his street, and

smoothed his hand over his hair. It had been cropped short in the nick, but he liked it that way and was going to keep it. He checked the tightness of the knot in his tie, glanced down at his zipper.

He felt good.

Flowers in one hand, chocolates in the other, he walked up the short pathway to the door of number 17. The tiny garden had been kept neat, the way he always liked it. The place needed a quick coat of paint, but it could wait another year. Two full dustbins stood by the door, one on each side, like guards.

Self-consciously, he rang the doorbell.

Flowers still in hand, he nervously brushed his stubbly hair again. A noise behind him made him turn. A small group of black youths were hanging around: one of them leaned on the gatepost, while the others were resting their backsides against cars. They were watching him, grinning at each other.

George turned back to the door.

He saw movement beyond the frosted glass window, a pale hand reaching up to turn the lock.

As the door opened, George's instant thought was that he had come to the wrong house, the wrong street. A girl stood there, a stranger to him: fair-skinned, fair-haired, slight of build, in that transitional moment between adolescence and womanhood, neither one nor the other but also both.

She was staring back at him, seeming to recognise him . . . but also scared.

She said: 'You want Mum?'

'Jeanie?' George said. 'Are you –?'

'*Mum!*' She had faced back into the house, her skinny hand still holding the brass ferruled knob of

5

the lock, an inch or two too high for her.

'Jeanie . . . listen!' George leaned towards her, and touched his forefinger to his lips. 'It's me! Shh. . . .'

'What do you want, then?'

He was transfixed by the sight of her: the last time he had seen her she was just a kid . . . seven, eight, mucky faced and crying, out in the garden at the back, sitting in the long grass, while the filth searched him, and Dawn screamed his stupidity at him. Suddenly that kid had become a woman, or was about to. He knew she would have grown up in seven years, but not like this . . . not *pretty*. He had expected – he hadn't thought about it. Just taken it for granted, his mind locked in the seven years of suspended animation. Jeanie!

'Who is it, Jeanie?'

Dawn appeared from the direction of the kitchen, wiping her hands absentmindedly down the front of her apron. Jeanie glanced back, then at George again. Her expression had changed: the confusion had gone. Now she showed fear. The door started to close.

George stepped forward, the flowers suddenly feeling loose in his hand.

Dawn saw him.

'Get inside, love,' she said to the girl, but Jeanie was frozen in place. Dawn elbowed her away. 'Get the hell out of here!' she shouted at George.

The door swung at him, but he kicked his foot forward and blocked it.

'I just want to talk to her!' he said.

'No.'

'Just for a minute, Dawn.'

'Jeanie, get inside!' She now had her weight on the

door, trying to force it against his foot. He could see past her: Jeanie was standing back in the hall, her arms hanging limply at her sides, staring at him, staring and staring. . .

'Mum . . . ?'

Dawn screamed, momentarily shocking him.

'Get *inside*!' she yelled.

'One minute, Dawn. I only want one minute. . .'

'She doesn't know you, George. She doesn't *want* to know you!'

She pulled back, easing the pressure on his foot, and George took the opportunity to shove his forearm against the door, forcing it open wider. But Dawn was only gathering strength: she threw her full weight against the door, almost managing to slam it and knocking the flowers out of his hand.

Irrationally, he grabbed them as they fell, snatching at the heads . . . and yellow petals sprayed around him.

'I'm only here to see her,' he shouted.

'You left it too damned long.'

'You can't do this to me!'

'You fucking *watch*!'

'She's my daughter too.' But Dawn was hysterical, and started to scream again.

For an instant he glimpsed Jeanie again, still stuck in horror, then he stood back. The door slammed on him.

It was the screaming that did it; he hated people to scream at him. He flung the battered bunch of daffodils at the door, and they scattered and fell.

'I wanted to say hello, you bloody cow!' he bawled at the unresponding door. 'That's all . . . bloody hello!'

He hurled the paper bag with the chocolates at the door; it missed, and bounced off the wall. George lunged forward, picked up one of the dustbins and raised it above shoulder height. The lid fell off behind him, and clattered on the ground. He slung the bin at the door with all his strength, aiming for the glass. It hit the frame, and crashed to the ground, spilling newspapers, cereal packets, tea leaves, potato peelings, the cardboard tube from a toilet roll.

He stepped back, panting.

'HELLO!' he shouted.

The rubbish bin was rolling towards him, bumping over its handles. George took a violent kick at it, spilling more garbage on the ground.

The door remained shut against him.

Still breathing heavily, he turned around, trying to think what to do next. To his surprise, he saw that a small crowd had gathered. The youths he had seen earlier were watching with keen interest.

'And you lot can fuck off too!' he said.

He set his shoulders belligerently, and went towards them. Most of the people stepped back, but the youths held their ground.

'Go on, fuck off!'

One of the blacks was leaning on the gatepost. George jabbed a finger towards him. 'Get off my gate.'

The kid was about eighteen, wearing a brightly coloured shirt and one of those immense peaked caps. He grinned insolently at George.

'Isn't your gate, man.'

George took two handfuls of shirt, and pulled the kid towards him.

'I said, get off my bleeding gate.'

'You gonna clean up that mess?'

For a moment George tasted naked, total anger . . . but he had already gone far enough.

Instead of hurting the kid, he said: 'That's what you're here for.'

The contempt in his voice was provocative enough. The kid moved expertly, and twisted away from his grip. He hooked an ankle behind George, punched him with both fists on the chest, and George fell back. Recovering, he swung around. The other two blacks were already behind him, ready for him. He lunged out at them, knocking off a cap, aiming for the face. From behind, the first youth had moved again, getting a strong forearm round George's neck, pulling back on his throat. One of the others punched him low. George broke free, raised a fist . . .

But a strong hand grabbed his arm, and another fended the black away.

A familiar voice said: '*Hey* . . . hey, hey!'

The scrapping continued for another few seconds, but Thomas was there now . . . huge Thomas.

'Come on, it's OK. Cool it, cool it.' The soft Glaswegian accent, the filthy overalls, the smell of motor oil and sweat. George felt calm spreading over him.

The black youths seemed surrounded by Thomas.

'Leave him alone, will you?' Thomas said. 'He's very upset.'

They jostled away, trying to save face, still looking aggressive but disarmed by Thomas. The incident was over. Thomas' great arm went around George's shoulders, and led him down the street.

George said: 'Where the hell did that lot come from?'

'They live here, George.'

'Since when?'

'Since you went inside. Things have changed.'

George glanced back: the crowd had dispersed, the youths had gone. The street looked the same as it always had . . . except now it was no longer his.

'That's the word, George, isn't it? Upset?'

'Upset is what I am.'

But he was very pleased to see Thomas.

Chapter 2

'Did you happen to get that last parcel I sent you?'

'Yeah,' George said. 'It shouldn't have been the driver, though.'

'Then who?'

'I pinned him in the first chapter.'

'Who was it?'

'The Chinese guy . . . the one who fed the goldfish.'

'You didn't write the book, George.'

'No . . . but if I had. . .'

They had walked a mile or so from the house. Thomas no longer had his arm around George's shoulder, but they were picking up again where they had left off. The old chummy feeling, easy familiarity, joshing each other about thrillers and what they ought to be doing with their lives.

George was thinking this was what he should have done first: gone and found Thomas, eased himself back into the old life nice and slow. He was too impetuous, but Jeanie had been on his mind. That bitch Dawn . . .

They were getting close to where Thomas had his place, and George was wondering what he was going to find there. Thomas always surprised him, and this time he'd had seven years to change things around a bit. Thomas called his place his studio, his only conceit, that he was some kind of artist; anyone else seeing Thomas' place would have called it a scrapyard. The local council would probably close it down . . . might even have done so already, for all he knew. But that old workshop, crammed under a railway arch, was the only place George could think of as home, at least for the time being.

Then he saw the Jaguar.

'Christ!' he said, unbelieving.

'What?' Thomas said.

'You kept it!'

' 'Course I did . . . thought you wanted me to.'

'Yeah . . . but I didn't think . . .'

It was parked on a yellow line, standing under a tree. George hurried over to it, marvelling that it was still the same.

It had recently been washed and polished, and the sun glinted from the yellow paint and gleaming chrome trim.

George tried the handle on the driver's side.

'You keep it tuned?'

'Need you ask? Just passed its MOT. New tyres, new tax disc, you name it.'

'Christ . . .' George said again, running his hand lightly over the paintwork. 'I never expected to see this again . . .'

Thomas was holding out a key ring. Suddenly very contented indeed, George took the keys from him and climbed inside the car. It smelled of old leather, just like it should. He reached over to touch each of the knobs on the dashboard, rattled the gear lever to and fro in neutral, then adjusted the rear-view mirror, first to look at himself in it, then to the right angle for driving.

Thomas had moved into the passenger seat. George started the engine – it fired first time, and settled into a powerful purring noise – and moved the Jaguar away from the kerb. He glanced at the instruments.

'You been clocking this, Thomas?'

'Why do you think that?'

'You haven't been doing much driving, according to the clock.'

'I told you I was looking after it. I don't have many places to drive to.'

'It's great, just great.'

He drove carefully and slowly for the first half-mile or so, then felt the old skills coming back. He just wanted to drive round and around, look at places all over again.

Then Thomas said: 'So if you'd written it, it would have been better.'

'Written what?'

'The book.'

'Oh . . . the book. See, he could have been feeding the goldfish and seen the second wife in the reflections in the goldfish bowl.'

'And cut the body up and fed it to the fish?'

'Yeah. Killer goldfish.'

Thomas made the familiar short snorting sound that came out when he found something funny.

'Don't laugh,' George said. 'I had a lot of time to think about all that.' With his free hand he rattled around in the ledge under the dashboard, until he found what he was looking for. 'Want a tape on?'

Thomas shrugged, but without waiting for a real

answer George slipped a cassette into the slot. The tape had already been partly played, and it came on in the middle of a track. Nat 'King' Cole came soothing out at them.

George took a deep, satisfied breath, straightening his arms and pressing his shoulders against the soft leather seat back.

'Why does she hate me like that, Thomas?'

'She doesn't.'

'Yes she does.'

'Can't tell with women, George. You never can. They're different, you know. They wear skirts. They like to powder their noses, and when they go to Heaven they get wings.'

'Like angels.'

'Yeah.'

'But angels are men,' George said.

'Men!' Thomas laughed again. 'No one told me that.'

'It's true. Angels are men.' He turned his head sharply to the side, looked at one of the shops they were passing, then braked and pulled over to the side. Thomas lurched forward and braced himself against the dash, turning his head to see what was going on. 'Bear that in mind, Thomas . . . angels are always men.'

He opened the car door, narrowly missing having it smashed off by a passing bus, then climbed out. A pet shop was there a few yards back, and he walked quickly towards it.

Inside was that smell of animals, vaguely suggestive of excrement and grain, several long racks of white-painted cages and an Indian man in a stained white coat.

Standing just inside the door, George said: 'You got any white rabbits with long floppy ears?'

In a voice totally uninfluenced by the mystic Orient, the Indian said: 'I got one called Arthur.'

'Is he white?'

'Yes . . . but he's got short ears.'

'He'll do. Let's have a look at him.'

Arthur cost him eight pounds, which was most of what he had left in his pocket. Back in the car he passed the rabbit to Thomas, who held it in his lap.

'You remember, then?' Thomas said.

'How could I forget? I remember *everything*.'

'George, things have changed while you've been away.'

'Not that much, they haven't.'

He started the car again and pulled out into the traffic, driving more purposefully than before. He was remembering everything, and now he remembered where he wanted to go.

Chapter 3

George stopped the car near the mouth of an alley in the seediest part of Soho, the warren of streets behind Shaftesbury Avenue. He wound down the window, and stared along at a neon sign flicking on and off at the far end. In the bare daylight the garish display over the doorway looked more inept than inviting. *Paradise Club*, on and off, on and off, a warning of shabbiness within to the punters who ought to know better, but who never did.

'You can't go in there, George,' Thomas said.

'Why not?'

'It's different.'

'And Mortwell?' George asked. 'Is he different too?'

'Very different.'

'We'll see.'

'A lot's been changing while you were away,' Thomas said. 'You're out of touch, the rules are new.'

'Don't give me that.'

'Anyway, what makes you think Mortwell is going to remember?'

George reached over and plucked the rabbit from Thomas' lap. The animal scrambled frantically in his arms, but he soothed it with a gentle stroke over its ears.

'He has to, doesn't he?' George said.

Before Thomas could reply he stepped out of the car and headed down the alley.

The door to the club was closed, but not locked. He let himself in, and followed the steps down to a sub-basement. The place smelt of last night's alcohol and other people's piss. It was gloomy inside, probably by design. If there had been a few more lights everyone would have seen the damp stains on the walls, the cheap, rickety furniture, the decor inherited from the previous tenants.

George moved across the cramped space of the floor, holding the rabbit under his arm, but keeping it out of sight. He collided with a table, scraping it across the uncarpeted floor, and this made the only other visible occupant of the room turn in his diretion.

It was a girl, sitting in a desultory way on one of the bar stools, toying with a drink in a tall glass. She had long blonde hair, and was wearing a skimpy halter-neck dress.

She saw George, and immediately lost interest in him.

'We're closed,' she said, wearily. 'Come back this evening.'

'It's OK,' George said. 'I'm here now.'

She turned away from him.

'Terry, tell him.'

There was a noise in the shadows, and presently a tall man with thinning hair came forward. He was wearing black trousers and a frilly white shirt, part of a dress suit, the disguise he wore in the evenings.

'Yeah, we're closed, sir,' he said.

'Hiya, Terry,' George said. 'How you gettin' on?'

He went to the bar and leant against it, holding the rabbit in his arm and stroking its back.

'What you doing here?' Terry said.

'I'll have a Bloody Mary . . . and he'll have some lettuce.'

'George?'

'That's me.'

'What the hell do you want?'

'Looking for Mortwell, Terry. You know . . . a bit of work, and all that?' He glanced around the run-down bar. 'What's all this you're doin' now?'

'You know.' Terry looked uneasy. 'You know how it is . . . whatever comes up.'

'It's a knocking shop, isn't it?'

'Come on, George . . .'

'So where is he?'

'Who?'

George levered himself away from the bar, and Terry made a quick movement. Not defensive, but alert for trouble . . . shifting weight, ready for a move.

'I told you: I'm looking for Mortwell,' George said.

'He's not around.'

'He must be somewhere.'

'Yeah . . . that's true. You'd better ask Dudley.'

He nodded his head back, towards a half-drawn curtain at the darker end of the bar. A door was visible beyond it.

'Thanks, Terry. You're a great help.'

He pushed past the man, and walked quickly across the bar. His eyes had adjusted to the gloom, and he stepped around the scattered tables and chairs with a feeling of unnecessary nimbleness. It was good to be out and getting around again; his body was coming alive.

He pushed the door open without knocking, and went through. Beyond was a small office, daylight glinting down from the alleyway above. Pictures of naked girls were hanging from the walls: not crumpet pictures, like in a calendar, but as if they were on display, part of the staff. A man was leaning rather awkwardly over a desk, jabbing in an undirected way at the keyboard of a computer.

He looked up as George went in, more from surprise at the intrusion than from interest about who it might be.

George said: 'You expecting me, Dudley?'

The man's thoughts were obviously still more on the computer than on him. He glanced abstractedly at the glowing screen. He was dressed oddly, to George's mind: he had always known Dudley in open-necked shirt and jeans, yet now he had somehow got himself into a suit.

'Did you know I was out?' George said.

'We suspected you might be, George.'

The computer suddenly gave out a beeping sound. The screen cleared, then a long string of figures scrolled up from the bottom and vanished into the oblivion beyond the top. Dudley reached over and hit a key, and the display instantly froze.

He grinned at George in an embarrassed way.

'To think we were once just honest villains,' he said. 'Now all this.'

'So where is he?'

'Where's who?'

'Leave it out, Dudley.'

'Mortwell's away. South of France.'

'Oh yeah?'

'Yeah. Things aren't easy, George. Nothing like they used to be.'

'He owes me, Dudley. Said he'd look after me.'

'He said a lot of things in the old days.'

'These are the new ones. He owes me.'

The rabbit was squirming in his arms, ears laid flat against its head, its little paws fighting against his arm.

'Well,' George said. 'If you see him, give him this.'

He thrust the rabbit across at Dudley, who, taken by surprise, accepted it. The rabbit nuzzled against him.

'He's called Arthur,' George said. 'And he likes lettuce.'

Not waiting for an answer, he pushed back through the door and returned to the main part of the shabby night club. Terry was standing at the bar talking to the girl, and they both ignored him.

He had reached the bottom of the steps when he heard Dudley's voice.

'George!'

He turned back.

'What?'

'We can talk.'

'You gonna waste my time again?'

Dudley replied by going back into the office. George followed him, feeling put upon but not sure why. By the time he got to the office a second time, Dudley was leaning over the computer again, partly crushing Arthur. George watched him, feeling impatient.

The monitor on the computer flickered purpose-fully, then seemed to jam up. Dudley bashed randomly at keys, without visible effect.

'Fuck these things anyway,' he said.

'What you trying to do?'

'Get back to the operating system.'

'Out of the way,' George said.

He reached past the man, and found what he was looking for on the keyboard. He pressed a couple of keys and the disk drive started turning. Arthur leapt out of Dudley's arms, and landed on the desk. He sniffed the side of the computer, then shuffled away.

The disk drive turned itself off and the screen cleared. The cursor blinked humbly at them both.

'Here, where did you learn to do that?' Dudley said.

'In the nick. They teach you all sorts of useful things these days. You should try it some time.'

'Ha very ha.'

'No, really . . .'

Dudley reached into his pocket. 'You know what this is, George?'

'It ain't one of them,' he said, meaning the computer.

'We have need of a driver. Take it.'

George took the object, a small black instrument, surprisingly heavy for its size, with a pocket clip like a pen.

'What is it?'

'It's a bleep. Keep it in your pocket. We'll call you.'

Chapter 4

People kept telling him the world had changed, but it hadn't. Not really. Superficial things, perhaps, but people were still the same. Mortwell still owed him, Dudley was an evasive bastard, Terry ran a clip joint . . . and Thomas still lived underneath the arches.

'You ain't never going to clean up, are you?' George said, squeezing past an immense pile of packing cases.

'I did, but you weren't here to see it.'

'When was that, then?'

'Two or three years ago.'

George said: 'Don't you go on reminding me, like everyone else.'

Thomas ignored him, reaching up to switch on an overhead light. The switch was on a long wire trailing from the ceiling miles above, and when he let it go it swung to and fro.

George looked around appreciatively, remembering the old days. Much of the chaotic jumble was exactly as he had last seen it, stacked high, leaning in precarious mountains in the dimmer corners of the workshop. A fire hazard is what it was, but it looked and felt like home. Bloody cold, though.

There was order in Thomas' chaos, in spite of his persistent attempts to fill the unfillable space. Somehow or other he had managed to get a small caravan into the workshop, and it was here he slept. George too, in the old days, when things had first gone wrong with Dawn. Now it seemed they had turned full circle again.

Along one side was the area Thomas referred to, in his heavy-handed jocular way, as his sitting room. In reality, a small space had been cleared for a couple of bucket seats from an old car. There was no room in the caravan for anything but sleeping, so all meals, and whatever there was of Thomas' social life, took place in the yawning cavern of the workshop.

They had been out and around London all day, and George was feeling tired. It had been a long day for someone who had grown used to days with twenty-three hours inside a cell.

'I've got something I want to show you,' Thomas said.

'I know what that means. Trouble.'

'Not this time, George. Have a look.'

He led George proudly to a cramped area tucked away behind the caravan, and switched on another light. A trestle table stood there precariously, loaded with what looked like two dozen plates of spaghetti.

'What do you think?' Thomas said.

'I think it looks like spaghetti.'

'Look more closely.'

Thomas picked up one of the plates, and handed it to him. George prodded at it nervously. It was soft and shiny, and had an authentically soggy texture. It was stone cold, and, when George touched it, dry.

'It's plastic,' Thomas said. 'The latest thing from Japan.'

'Do you melt it down and eat it?'

'No . . . it's ornamental.'

'Ornamental *spaghetti*?'

'Yeah. It's going to go like a bomb.'

'You reckon? Where do you go out and get plastic spaghetti from?'

Thomas tapped a knowing finger against the side of his nose.

'Contacts, George,' he said. 'You've got to have contacts in the art world.'

Thomas said he was going to cook some dinner, so George sat around for a while, thinking about Jeanie and thinking about Mortwell. He took the bleep out of his pocket and looked at it.

'You ever seen one of these things before?' he called to Thomas.

Thomas' head materialised from behind a crate. He had a smudge of red paste by his mouth.

'It's a pager,' he said.

'Dudley called it a bleep.'

'He would. It's an auto-pager. It means they can send out a radio message anywhere in London, and it'll make a noise, and you'll know they want you.'

'I sussed that out for myself. But how does it work . . .? I mean, it hasn't even got an aerial.'

'It doesn't need one. I'll show you.'

Thomas came out from behind the crate holding a metal ladle. He made George hold out the pager in his hand, then touched something on the back. The thing let out a wild electronic wailing noise, so loud and so suddenly that George almost dropped it.

'Bloody hell!'

'You can turn the volume down . . . that's just a test circuit.' Thomas fiddled with it, then handed it back. 'Change the batteries once a month, and don't mess with Mortwell.'

'Is that a warning?'

'It's advice from an old pal.'

'He owes me this.'

'I thought you said he wasn't in it.'

'He's not – You know.'

'No, I don't.' Thomas waved his ladle in the air in a circular motion. 'Excuse me, George old pal . . . I've got work to do.'

'They said he was in France,' George called towards the space behind the crate. 'He doesn't even know I'm out yet.'

Thomas didn't answer.

Later he said, from behind the crate: 'There's a present for you there.'

'Where?'

'On one of the chairs. A book.'

George picked it up: it was a paperback omnibus edition of the novels of John Franklin Bardin.

'Thanks, Thomas. Is it any good?'

Thomas appeared, carrying two plates of steaming hot food. He gave one of them to George.

'Here you go.'

'Thanks,' George said again, then did a double take. 'What's this? Spaghetti?'

'It's good for you. Build you up.'

'Is it real?'

'I told you it'd catch on.' Thomas sat down, and started forking food into his mouth. 'The book's about opera singers. Somebody's murdering them, and after every murder they leave a Percheron.'

'What's a Percheron?'

'It's a kind of horse.'

'You mean the big white horse that pulls the milk cart?'

'Something like that.'

'And?' George said.

'And then it gets complicated.'

'Sounds complicated enough already.'

'You like complications, though, don't you?'

'Only in books,' George said. He rested a heavy elbow on the open spine of the book, and started to read while he ate.

The following day, around four in the afternoon, George drove his yellow Jaguar slowly down a side-street in Wandsworth. There was no room to park, so he stopped in the road, letting the engine idle.

On his right was a long row of terraced houses, all basically the same, but each one customised in trivial ways to reflect the idiosyncrasies of the owners. There were arrangements of glassed-in porches, imitation stone cladding, unusual colour schemes on the paint-work, and so on. On the other side, topping a long brick wall, was a high fence of the sort of net they put around tennis courts. It reminded George of the prison, yet he took pleasure in knowing not only that it wasn't, but that anyway he was here, outside, in his own car.

A moment or two after four, the schoolchildren started pouring out . . . both sexes, all sizes, and representatives of every conceivable member-state of the United Nations. George's interest perked up, and he scanned the young faces as they milled past his car.

He soon saw her, walking along silently with a group of her friends, her eyes cast towards the ground. He thought she looked tired; perhaps Dawn had been giving her a hard time because of what had happened the previous morning.

As Jeanie passed the car, George looked anxiously towards her, hoping to catch her eye. But she failed to look at him, and he was too uncertain of what would follow to call to her.

In a few moments she was lost to his sight in the crowds of other children.

Then his balls let out a wailing cry, and he jumped with alarm.

Instantly knowing what it was, he swore to himself and felt around in his trousers pocket. He found the pager, and switched it off.

After a short drive he lucked across the one remaining phone-box in London that hadn't been vandalised, and called the number Dudley had given him. A man's voice simply said: 'We got work for you,' and then hung up.

Chapter 5

George had to call Dudley to get the address, but at last he found the place: a semi-detached house in an ordinary suburban street in Harlesden. When he knocked on the door there was a long silence. It opened after his second knock.

The woman who answered said: 'In there.'

It was a typical front parlour: feeling cold and seeming unused. The furniture smelt musty. Standing by the door was a huge cardboard carton that had once carried South African apples.

George tried to lift it, but he could barely raise a corner. The woman stood there and watched.

'Am I expected to carry this bleeding thing on my own?' he said.

'You brought a car, didn't you?'

George gritted his teeth, and managed somehow to get the thing into his arms, out of the house and into the approximate vicinity of the car. Here he discovered that he had, with immense foresight, left the boot locked up. He had to put the carton down again while he unlocked and opened it, then hefted it somehow into the space within.

The woman was still standing there watching him.

'Where to?' he said.

'The address is on it.' She turned to go back into the house. 'You can read, I suppose?'

The door slammed against him, against the world. Muttering, George manhandled the carton around until he found the address pencilled on the side.

The drop was a porno video shop near King's Cross, the sort that had a warning about adult material written on a small placard near the door. A youth from somewhere in the Middle East was waiting beside a makeshift desk inside the garishly lit interior. When George arrived he simply gestured with a movement of his head that the package should be taken into the inner office, beyond the screen of plastic hanging beads.

When he had dumped it, George said: 'What now?'

'I dunno.'

'Don't you want to sign for it, or something?'

'You got something for me to sign?'

'Nah.' George glared at him, and departed.

Later that evening, George left his Jaguar in the car park of a fancy hotel in Cumberland Gate, and walked curiously towards the revolving door of the main entrance.

A commissionaire in green livery was standing there, a shiny top hat balanced on his elegant head, a pair of white gloves held obscurely in his right hand. George had noticed this before: the flunkeys who stood outside posh hotels always held their gloves, never wore them. One day he'd ask one of them why.

As he passed, the commissionaire murmured: 'Good evening, sir.'

'Good evening,' George said, wondering if he was after a tip.

The doorman then looked rather pointedly down at

George's shoes; in response, George looked pointedly down at *his*. (They were impeccably black and glossy; George's were . . . well, just the ones he always wore.)

Puzzled by all this, George revolved through the doors and into the main lobby.

He looked around with interest: at one end was the reception area, staffed by three fastidiously groomed young women. Two porters stood on duty in an office behind the desk. In a small arcade beyond there were several small shops: a furrier's, a jewellery store, a perfumery and a news-stand. A few glass cases stood against the walls containing gloves, leather goods and glassware.

This commercial zone, though, was but a small part of the whole. The lobby was obviously the main meeting-point and thoroughfare of the hotel, because numerous small tables with attendant chairs were arranged in discreetly screened areas, surrounded by large potted indoor plants, while the thickly carpeted hall led through columned arches to a number of different areas of the hotel: there were signs to at least two restaurants, a tea room, the lifts, and so on. In the middle of the lobby was a grand double staircase, the bannisters gilded and the stair rods gleaming, and hanging from the ceiling above the stairwell was an immense crystal chandelier.

Somewhere in the near distance, a trio was playing nostalgic melodies.

Seeing a white-coated waiter, George walked up to him.

'Is there a bar in this place?' he said.

The waiter, a good-looking young man with aquiline features, looked politely at him.

'If you would care to take a seat, sir, I shall be pleased to serve you.'

'OK, then . . . I'll have a Bloody Mary.'

'Take a seat, sir.'

George frowned, then backed away. He saw a table where no one was sitting, and walked over to it. He felt suddenly self-conscious, and was acutely aware that he didn't fit in this place. Mustering as much grace as he could, he sat down, folded one leg over the other, and looked intently towards the waiter.

The young man walked over.

'Something to drink, sir?'

'I told you . . . Bloody Mary.'

'Yes of course, sir. With sauce?'

'Yeah. With sauce.'

The waiter scribbled something on a pad, resting it on his silver tray, then walked away with a measured tread. George noticed that his hair was drawn back into a small pigtail, tied with an elastic band. Waiters had pigtails now?

The drink came sooner than he expected, placed in front of him on a paper serviette. As soon as the waiter had left him, George picked up the glass and drank quickly. He looked around, wondering who was going to meet him.

He noticed that a man in a dark suit had walked slowly past his table a couple of times, looking at him suspiciously. The second time, George grinned and raised his glass to him.

Four Arabs paraded through the lobby, trailed by a number of veiled women. When they had passed, exotic perfumes wafted behind.

'Something more to drink, sir?'

The waiter had reappeared, no later than four seconds after he had emptied his glass.

'Yeah . . . same again, please.'

'And this time?'

'What about this time?'

'With or without?' the waiter said, his ballpoint raised.

'With,' said George.

'Thank you, sir.'

Once again, the drink materialised before him in a matter of seconds. George imagined a big tap behind the bar, marked Bloody Mary.

'That will be four pounds twenty, sir.'

'What makes you think I'm finished?'

'There's no hurry, sir.'

George fished into his pocket and found a five-pound note. He handed it to the waiter, who made a big production of searching rather slowly for the change. George waited him out, and watched as his eighty pence of change was counted into his hand.

'Thanks,' George said, slipping it into his pocket.

'Thank *you*, sir.'

The waiter resumed his station in the central area of the lobby, and George resumed his expectant wait. Sipping at his drink, he realised he was glimpsing a style of life he was not normally privy to: the milieu of businessmen, visiting Arabs, wealthy tourists. What was more, the representatives of this lifestyle were well aware he was an intruder. Numerous disparaging glances (subtly veiled, but unmistakable) came his way, and the man in the dark suit, whom George had now identified as being probably the hotel detective, continued to keep a well-trained eye on him.

His drink was only half-finished when George saw something that interested him.

A movement at the top of the wide staircase caught his eye. A slim young woman had appeared along the upper landing, walking quickly towards the stairs. At first glance from this low angle she appeared to have no clothes on (hence his interest), but as she came fully into view George could see she was wearing a tiny strapless dress, covered in glittering blue diamanté. At the head of the stairs she paused to pull on a voluminous grey overcoat, far too big for her, but effectively covering her slim body and the diminutive dress.

She came quickly and purposefully down the stairs. She was black and beautiful, her long frizzy hair drawn into a free-flowing bundle on the side above her left ear. She had the natural-seeming poise of the professional model, and moved with a grace that survived the haste of her passage down the stairs. George stared at her with vague lust: since coming out she was the first woman he had seen that he fancied.

Yet he also knew that she was permanently beyond his reach: she had style, quality and innate class. He was in his middle forties, had prison-cropped hair, was uncouth and graceless . . . and his lust remained vague because what he really felt was a pang of hopelessness.

So he watched her in the way a man will, when he knows that she will always belong to another.

But when she reached the lobby she glanced in his direction and walked quickly towards him.

When she was only a few feet away from him, she was neatly intercepted by the house detective.

'You doing business here?' he said, quietly but very distinctly.

The young woman ignored him, and tried to brush past him. The detective persisted.

'Madame, can I help you?'

He had gripped her elbow, but she wrenched it away from him with an angry gesture. She stepped past him and descended on George, a bright smile forcing its way across her face.

'Darling! Nice of you to wait . . . I'm so sorry I kept you!'

She bent towards him and planted a juicy kiss full on his lips.

George could see the detective hovering just behind her.

He said quietly: 'What's with the "darling", then?'

The girl took his arm, and gestured him to stand up. George complied, feeling confused. She held herself against him affectionately, and whispered in his ear: 'For fuck's sake!'

'What . . .?'

'Let's go, darling!' she said out loud. 'We're going to be late!'

Her fingernails were biting into his arm while she steered him towards the main door, but her face retained its happy smile. People stared.

They got through the revolving door with some awkwardness, it not having been designed for two people to go through simultaneously. As they passed the commissionaire he nodded to them politely. For old time's sake, George sneaked in another pointed look at the man's shoes.

'Where's the car?' the girl said.

34

'The Jag . . . over there.'

He moved away from her, but she caught his arm again.

'Pretend you know me!' she said quietly, but angrily.

'I don't know you . . . darling.'

'Then pretend you fucking do!'

When they reached the car, George opened the rear passenger door for her. She reached past him and slammed it shut.

'Not the back! I get in the front!'

'Suit yourself.'

He walked around to the driver's door, climbed in, and then opened the passenger door from inside. The girl slid in beside him.

'Where the hell did they get *you* from?' she said.

'Under a cabbage leaf.'

She stared out of the window, back towards the hotel. The commissionaire was staring at them.

'Drive . . . would you?' she said.

Chapter 6

'Next time . . . be ready for me!' the girl said.

'Do you mind explaining what all that was about?'

'Get going.'

'OK . . . but where to?'

'I have to work these places,' she said. 'The staff turn a blind eye, but the manager doesn't.'

'Will you tell me where you want to go?'

'The Lambert.'

'At last,' George sighed. He accelerated away, and swung into the road. A car was coming the other way, and he swerved to avoid it. The girl was thrown against the door of the car.

'*Jesus!*' she cried.

'Sorry.'

She was still furious with him. She said: 'Didn't they tell you that you're meant to be my date, not my minicab driver?'

'They told me nothing. What's your date supposed to do?'

'He looks after me, you dingbat! He's meant to want to see me.'

'And what if he doesn't?'

'He pretends.'

'How does he pretend?'

'Christ! Who *sent* you?'

'Does it matter? It's just a job . . . darling.'

'Shut up and drive, would you?'

Suppressing a number of sharp rejoinders, George shut up and drove. The girl switched on the interior light, and swivelled his rear-view mirror so she could see herself. She combed her hair, flicked gloss over her lips, peered closely to check her eye make-up.

'Anyway, what's your name?' George said.

'None of your damned business.'

He took a deep breath, then expelled it, repenting of yet another retort.

In a moment he said: 'My name's George.'

'So what?'

'Look . . . I got to call you *something*.'

'I don't see why. You can call me Simone.'

'Is that your real name?'

'It's what you call me. OK?'

'OK, Simone.'

Satisfied with that, but not entirely, George concentrated on his driving. In the end she even let him have his mirror back.

An hour or so later he was sitting boredly in the bar of the Lambert, a Bloody Mary in front of him, when Simone reappeared.

He said: 'You want a drink?'

'No. Let's go.'

George drained his glass, then stood up. 'As you wish, dear.'

He took her arm and they walked towards the exit.

'Is this how you like it?' George said, as people glanced curiously at them.

He heard her suck in her breath, very irritated with

him. George suppressed the wish to break something over her head.

Back in the car, he said: 'Where to now?'

'St John's Wood.'

'St John's Wood, please?'

'You heard. Get going.'

George sighed, and drove away. When he had got past Marble Arch he reached forward and slid his tape into the player. Nat 'King' Cole started singing *Mona Lisa*.

'Turn it off, would you?'

'Don't you like it?'

'I just don't want to hear it.'

'Whose bloody car is this, anyway?'

'At the moment it's mine.' She reached down and hit the eject button.

His hands tightened angrily on the steering wheel, but he said nothing. Minutes passed.

Then he said: 'So how many do you do in an evening?'

'Do you want your face slapped?'

'Just making polite conversation.'

'Then don't.' She took a cigarette from her bag. 'Give me a light, please.'

George pressed in the automatic lighter in the fascia, and when it popped out he handed it to her.

'You working for Mortwell too?' he said.

'I'm with the agency, if that's what you mean.'

'What agency?'

'The one that sent me you.' She peered at the passing houses. 'You turn right here, then next on the left.'

George was impressed, in spite of everything. They

were in the sort of residential area that made you feel you needed a million quid in your pocket, even to drive down the road.

'I thought we were looking for another hotel,' he said.

'No. In here.'

It was a large detached house set well back from the road at the end of a gravel drive. Following Simone's directions he parked the car to the side of the house, in an area where the gravel had been laid in a wide apron.

As soon as he had turned off the engine, Simone opened her door and got out. Looking back at him, she said: 'Fifteen.'

'What . . . hours or minutes?'

She made no reply and stepped briskly towards the house.

George watched curiously. As she approached the door it was opened from within, and a servant in a white suit stood there. He inclined his head slightly as she passed, then closed the door.

He looked for a while longer, hoping there would be more to see. At one point two vague shadows were briefly visible against a curtained window, but then nothing more. George slotted his tape back into the player, and settled back to wait.

His next awareness was of Simone tapping angrily on his window. George jerked awake, ejected the tape, then leaned over to hold the door for her. This time she chose to sit in the back seat.

The door to the house closed as he started the engine.

'That was quick,' he said.

'You were asleep.'

'Was I?'

'Don't sleep. You're meant to look after me.'

'I thought I was just the driver . . . or possibly your date.'

He took the car into the sidestreet, and headed back towards the main road.

'Where to now?' he said.

'King's Cross.'

They passed Lord's Cricket Ground, and George turned left, circling the northern side of Regent's Park towards Camden Town.

'So how was he?' he said.

Simone made no reply. She was fussing with her hair once more.

'How was the Arab?'

Again she ignored him.

Irritated, George swerved suddenly into a side road, making her lurch across the back seat.

'Not so damned fast!' she yelled.

'You're still there, then?' he said.

'Just take me where I want to go, and quit asking questions.'

'OK, OK.'

He approached King's Cross from the north, along the network of low streets between old warehouses and under the profusion of Victorian railway bridges.

'Go right here,' Simone said, and George complied. They came into a narrow street built on a bridge over the wide approaches to the platforms. During the days this would be somewhere to look for an unused parking meter, or a short cut to the station if you were walking, but now it was night and the mean street had been taken over.

Provocatively dressed prostitutes leaned against

the bridge parapet at regular intervals, while others stood in pairs by the side of the kerb. A few cars were driving slowly along the street, and some of these had stopped; the drivers spoke to the women through the open window on the passenger side.

'This is a bit down-market for you, isn't it?' George said.

'Ssh!'

George sat in resentful silence, watching the illicit trade go on. It seemed to him that most of the whores were very young . . . they were dolled up to the nines, their faces lost behind a mask of lurid make-up, but their slim girlish figures still had some of the gawkiness of adolescence. He could not avoid thinking of Jeanie; he could have sworn that half the girls here were roughly the same age.

He looked in the rear-view mirror to see what Simone was doing, and to his surprise saw that she was leaning forward intently, staring at the girls.

The arrival of his car could not go unnoticed, and after a few moments one of the prostitutes eased herself away from the wall and headed towards them. George saw her in the beam of his headlights: she was dressed in a schoolgirl uniform, a parody of a parody, a girl disguised as a woman disguised as a child.

Simone said sharply: 'Drive on, please.'

'You sure?'

'I said drive on!'

'Whatever you say, dearest.'

He complied, and as they passed the prostitute she abandoned her childlike pose, and raised two fingers towards them.

'Friends of yours?' George said.

No answer.

Following her reluctant directions, George drove to Islington, a short distance away, and brought the car to a halt outside a modern block of flats. Simone made no move.

'What now?'

'You leave me here,' she said.

'Goodnight, then.'

He heard her fumbling in her bag, and then she leaned forward and pushed something towards him.

'Here . . . take this. Get yourself some clothes.'

'*Clothes?* What's wrong with this lot?'

'If you're going to drive me, you need new clothes.' She nudged his shoulder with her hand. 'Use this.'

It was a wad of banknotes. George curled his lip and looked away.

'You can't pay me,' he said.

'Why not?'

'You don't even like me.'

'That doesn't matter a damn. I can claim it.' She forced the notes into his hand. 'Goodnight.'

Then she was gone, slamming the door behind her.

Chapter 7

'Where are you up to?' Thomas said, ladling scrambled eggs on to George's plate.

George looked up from the book.

'I'm at the place where the dwarf loses his memory and wakes up in the police station.'

'Have you come to the bit where he finds the horse in his bedroom?'

'No.'

'Ah,' said Thomas. 'The best is yet to come.'

'It'd better be soon.'

George began eating appreciatively. He had always liked Thomas' cooking: plain grub, cooked plain.

'So what's the job?'

'You know . . . driving. That sort of thing.'

'Driving what?'

'My car. Very demanding.'

'Who or what is in the car?'

'A tall, thin, black tart,' George said, relishing the phrase. 'I could write a book, you know.'

'Too many T's.'

George looked up from his food. 'There's a B in it too.'

'Still too many T's.'

'He comes out of the nick, see . . . and they owe him one. So they give him a job driving a tall, thin, black tart. She hates him, treats him like a doormat –'

'And he hates her?' Thomas said.

'Well, kind of.'

'You mean he likes her?'

'He doesn't fucking know her, does he?'

The auto-pager bleeped, hanging in his jacket a few inches from his head. George jumped, and spluttered on his mouthful of food.

'There's your tart,' said Thomas.

'Too early in the day for her,' George said, wiping his mouth.

After a busy day, most of which was spent humping crates of porno videos around London, George was in the lounge of yet another expensive hotel, toying with a Bloody Mary. Although his back was aching, and he was nurturing a healthy hatred of the creepy denizens of the video world, he felt good. During what he had decided to call his lunch break, George had spent virtually all the money Simone had given him, and he was now decked out fit to be seen on the arm of a whore.

Fashions had changed while he was inside, so he had chosen conservatively, going for the clothes he liked the look of, not what any young git of a salesman tried to palm him off with. George had chosen a rakish leather bomber jacket and tight-fitting trousers, rounding off the effect with a flowery shirt and a pair of high-gloss Italian shoes.

Even so, the staff in the hotel were still giving him gyp, and the clientele seemed to shun him.

Simone arrived, and he turned to meet her.

'Sweet Jesus!' she breathed.

'What do you think?'

She simply shook her head.

'Don't you like them?' George said.

'Do you?'

'I bought them, didn't I?'

'You bought them all right.'

George squeezed his fingers into the back pocket of his trousers, and brought out some money.

'Anyway, here's your change,' he said.

'Not *here*, for God's sake!'

She took his arm, swung him around and propelled him towards the door. Once they were past the doorman she started in on him again.

'You know what? You're as much cover as a pair of fishnet tights and a leather miniskirt! I might as well have a sign round my neck. French model . . . cash on delivery.'

Brooding, George opened the passenger door for her, then went around to his own side. There was never any way of doing right with her. He felt offended and hurt . . . he'd tried to please her, even impress her a little. He remembered the first time he'd worn clothes like these, hanging out around the pubs and billiards halls in the Mile End Road, the recognised setter of style in his group. In those days no girl was safe from him. They liked him, liked the way he cut a dash. Twenty years ago. . . .

Maybe that was it. Twenty years, minus seven. Or was it plus?

He started the engine.

Simone was still worked up. She said: 'I could've killed you when I saw you! Look at you . . . got up like some fucking ponce! All you're missing is the gold medallion!'

George drooped, and let out a sigh. He reached down into the open neck of his shirt, pulled at the little gold chain and withdrew the medallion for Simone to see.

She glared at him, and turned away.

'So let's get this clear,' George said. 'You don't like medallions.'

'No, I do not.'

'And you don't like anything.'

'I hate every fucking thing about you!'

'OK sister, we got that straightened out.'

He was now violently angry, with her, with himself, with every damned thing. He crashed the car into gear, revved up the engine and drove into the street regardless of everything. Simone said nothing, watching the road with steely eyes.

'You see, I'm cheap,' George said bitterly. 'I can't help it. God made me cheap.'

'Being cheap is one thing. Looking cheap is another. That *really* takes talent.'

'And some women are whores. Some whores are black. We take what we're given, don't we?'

'I'm good at what I do. You're lousy at everything.'

'Listen, tart . . . I didn't ask for the privilege of driving you around. I was given you. Just like you didn't ask for me. The only difference is, you fucking complain all the time and I don't.'

He reached forward and jammed the tape into the player. *Mona Lisa* came on again, and George turned the volume up loud.

'Turn it off!' Simone said.

'No.'

'You heard me! Turn it off!'

Instead, he reached forward and pushed the volume up to full.

Shouting over the noise, he said: 'You asked me to buy clothes. I bought them. You tell me where to go, what to do. No please, no thank you. Do this, do that. You make remarks. And you're just a bloody whore.'

'Shut up!'

'Didn't nobody ever teach you manners?'

'You want to go on working for me?' Simone shouted.

'No.'

He jammed on the brakes, and the cars behind him had to swerve to avoid him. They were in Park Lane, six lanes of traffic jostling to get into the Hyde Park Corner interchange. Horns blared, and a taxi driver shouted something at them.

George ejected the tape.

'Get out!' he said. She looked at him, suddenly alarmed. 'Get fucking out of my car, lady!'

She stayed put, but said nothing. George threw his door open, ignored the cars brushing by, and strode around to the passenger side. He pulled her door wide open.

She stayed stubbornly inside, staring angrily ahead. George wasted no more time. He grabbed her arm and pulled her out into the street. She stumbled, and had to drop a hand to the ground to prevent herself falling. As she did so, the shapeless grey overcoat fell open, and in the glare of the passing headlights George saw for the first time that evening what she was wearing underneath. He caught a fleeting glimpse of a minuscule bra, black lace panties and bright-red suspenders.

She recovered, and hugged the coat around her. They stood there, facing each other, quivering with rage.

'OK,' George said. 'Now tell me I'm fired.'

She had tears of anger in her eyes.

'All right . . . you're fired, you bastard!'

'Lovely. Just what I wanted. Well, I'm fired, but you're street walking!'

He turned his back on her and walked jauntily around to his door.

As he got in she was still standing there, her face contorted with fury.

'You swine . . . you fucking swine!' she shouted.

George slammed the door, and drove away. He glanced in his rear-view mirror, and saw her still standing in the middle of the cars, a defiant survivor. In a moment, the dense traffic brought him to a halt, and he craned his neck to see her again. Her posture had abruptly changed: the defiance had been there for him to see so long as she thought he could see her. Now she looked crumpled and forlorn, a slim, vulnerable figure wandering precariously through traffic.

George remained angry, and she evoked no sympathy in him. When the traffic moved he lost sight of her, and he entered the mêlée of Hyde Park Corner with no greater intent than to find Thomas and spend the rest of the evening getting pissed.

He had reached the far side of the roundabout, where the traffic swings perilously round towards Knightsbridge, when he remembered that glimpse of what Simone was wearing under her coat. Irrationally, anger mixed with a feeling of guilt, and then became clouded with erotic thoughts: a young woman –

whatever her profession – wandering the streets of London, half-naked, as angry and upset as he was feeling, capable of any perverse act of self-destruction.

He sighed to himself, and continued on around the intersection before heading back up Park Lane.

He saw her almost at once. She had managed, somehow, to climb over the awkward metal barriers that divided the road down the centre, and was now trying to get across to the other side. She dashed in front of him, and he saw her slim legs breaking through the folds of the coat.

He swung the car over to the side, and got out.

She noticed him at once, and turned sharply away.

'Come on, Simone,' he said. He went up to her and touched her shoulder, but she wrenched it away from him. 'You can't stay out here.'

'Fuck off, George!'

'Come on . . . please. I'm sorry.'

'I'm all right. Leave me alone.'

'No, you're not. You can't walk about in London dressed like that.'

She looked at him then, and he saw that her expression had softened.

'Is my bag still in the car?' she said.

'Yeah . . . yes, of course it is!' He made a quick turn, and opened the rear passenger door. 'Your car awaits, Madame.' He realised what he had said. 'I mean –'

'I know what you mean.'

But, unexpectedly, she afforded him a brief smile.

'Come on then, Simone.'

At last she relented entirely, and climbed with some grace into the back seat of the car. He closed the door on her with as much delicacy as he could muster.

Back in the driving seat, George said: 'All right. Are we still in business together?'

'Don't rush it, George. Just drive me where I want to go.'

'Name the place.'

'You could put your music on, if you like.'

George grinned. 'You mean it?'

'Yes.'

He pushed in the tape: *Mona Lisa* blared out at full volume, and even he winced. He quickly ejected the tape.

'Thanks,' Simone said.

'So where do you want to go?'

'White's Hotel.'

George drove.

There was no car park at White's, so George had to find a place in the road outside.

'I'll be about twenty minutes,' Simone said. 'Will you mind all this for me?'

She gave him a loose handful of stuff, which he took in both hands. Several dozen banknotes were part of it all.

'What's this for?'

'Part of your job,' she said. 'I can't be found with a couple of hundred quid and a packet of rubbers in my handbag. Like you said, I'm a black whore.'

When she had gone, George slipped everything into the glove compartment, then had second thoughts and decided to sit with it all on his lap.

When Simone returned, she added more money to the pile.

'That's right,' she said. 'Leave it out where every-body can see it.'

George sighed, and put the lot into the glove com-partment.

'Where to?' he said.

'St John's Wood.'

George glanced at her with interest. 'Oh.'

'You'd better put your skates on. I'm running late.'

Half an hour later, George was sitting in the car on the gravel apron outside the house, and once again he had drifted off into a light doze. He dimly heard the sound of even footsteps on the gravel, and forced himself awake, not wanting to suffer her wrath yet again.

But it was not Simone: the servant in the white suit had walked to the car, and as George tried to collect his thoughts the man tapped politely on the window.

George wound it down.

'Madame thought you might like some refresh-ments, sir,' the man said in perfectly modulated English.

'Oh . . . all right. I mean, er . . . what is it?'

'Tea and sandwiches.'

'Thank you.' He took the tray through the window, and the servant politely inclined his head before turn-ing away.

'Um . . . will she be long?' George said.

'No more than usual, sir.'

'I see.'

The servant returned to the house, and closed the door. Goerge balanced the tray on his knees, and turned on the interior light. The tea and milk were in silver pots; the cup and saucer were of the finest bone china; and the sandwiches were on a plate with a design in gold leaf.

Surreptitiously, hoping no one in the house was watching him, George sniffed at the tea, and peeled up a corner of a sandwich to see what was inside. Ordinary tea; chicken sandwiches. Well, well . . .

He wolfed it all down, and had a second cup of tea.

By the time he had finished George noticed lights coming on in downstairs rooms of the house, so he brushed the crumbs off his lap and checked his appearance in the mirror. There remained the problem of the tea-tray; he could hardly take it with him in the car, and he didn't think he should leave it on the drive.

He got to the door of the house just as it opened. Simone was there, clad in her grey overcoat, but she was standing with a man George had not seen before. He was short and swarthy, had shining black hair and a neat, pointed beard.

They both stared at him.

George said: 'I didn't know, er, what to do with the tray . . .'

'I'll take it,' the Arab said, smiling in a way that simultaneously infuriated George and put him at his ease.

'All right, then.' He passed the tray over, wondering where the servant had gone. He tried to see beyond the man, into the interior of the house, but Simone took his arm and wheeled him around.

Without so much as a backward glance she walked him back to the car.

Driving down through St John's Wood High Street, George said: 'Is he the man you . . . see?'

'Yes.'

'He took his time this evening.'

Simone said nothing.

'Fall asleep halfway through?'

'Him or me?'

'Him,' George said. He glanced at her, and saw she was smiling. 'Well, you never know with these darkies, do you?'

She drew in her breath sharply. 'Thanks!'

'Sorry,' he said, meaning it. 'Told you I was cheap.'

'You fucking are, you know.'

George shook his head ruefully. 'Where are we going now?'

'King's Cross.'

'Back to the meat rack? Your wish is my command.'

She was searching in her bag, and in a moment she produced a cigarette. George reached over promptly, and made the dashboard lighter work.

'Thanks,' said Simone.

'See, I'm learning.'

'So am I.' She inhaled smoke, then watched through the window as the solid, respectable houses around Regent's Park gave way to the shabbier buildings that lay to the north of the station.

'Jesus, they're so *young*!' George said.

'Not all of them. Some whores go on until a grand old age.'

Her voice was abstracted, remote. She was sitting low in the seat, peering intently out at the street on the bridge.

'Tell me something,' George said.

'What?'

'Do they ever want you back?'

'Who?'

'Your clients.'

'Always.'

'Thought they might,' George said. 'They fall for you, then?'

Simone made no reply. She was watching as a prostitute stepped forward from the shadows and spoke to a man who had drawn up in a car.

'You didn't answer,' George said.

'Ssh!'

In the dim light of the street the prostitute looked young and fragile, and had a girlish tilt of the head as she negotiated with the driver. But another car went past, its headlights playing across her face . . . and suddenly the negotiations broke off. The man drove away, and the prostitute returned resignedly to the parapet of the bridge. She stood now where the light from an overhead lamp fell, and here she looked much older, more haggard, more used.

A black man went up to her, and put an arm around her shoulder.

'See, she found someone else.'

'Fool!' Simone said. 'That's her pimp.'

George stretched his limbs, disliking the rules of the game Simone seemed always to be playing, the one in which he was invariably in the wrong.

'Time to go,' Simone said.

'Anything you say.' He engaged gear, and drove down towards Euston Road. 'You didn't answer. Do they fall for you?'

'Sometimes. Sometimes they fall for what they think I am.'

'What's that?'

'What you think I am. A black whore.'

'Did I ever say that?'

'Yes. About an hour and a half ago.'

'I didn't mean it.'

'What do you think I am, then?' Simone said.

'Well, you're not a night nurse.'

'No, I'm not a nurse.'

'Let's say you're a lady.'

'Thank you, George. That'll do.'

He had reached the traffic lights at the front of King's Cross Station. 'Left or right?'

'Left.' She bit her lip. 'Please.'

They drove towards Islington, and another night's work was completed.

Chapter 8

It was Saturday, and George slept late, tucked up in the spare bunk in Thomas' caravan. When he emerged he found Thomas struggling with a consignment of cardboard boxes that had been delivered flat and unassembled from somewhere. There was some technique by which you flexed and pushed simultaneously, and the thing miraculously formed itself into a box. At least in theory. It was just that Thomas had not yet mastered the technique.

'Any chance of breakfast?' George said.

'Two hours ago. Hang around for lunch . . . you might be lucky.'

'What you doing?'

'Packaging.'

'The spaghetti?'

'When you've got the right product, you have to know how to sell it.' Thomas flexed another carton, but this time the triangular flaps that made up the base hung open. 'By the way, your pager keeps bleeping.'

'It's Saturday . . . my day off.'

'That's what I thought, so I didn't wake you.'

'There's no point me going out today . . . the video shops are all closed in the West End.'

'It might be her.'

'Who?'

'Three T's and a B.'

'That's evenings only.'

But the pager went again a few minutes later, and it was her. Grumbling, George started the car and drove to the address she gave him, near Piccadilly.

Chapter 9

She was waiting for him on a street corner, but
George drove past her once without recognising her.
She was wearing a modest skirt and jacket, and her
wild and exotic hair had been combed back and was
held with a simple clip. She had an ordinary handbag
on her arm, and looked for all the world like a secretary waiting to meet her boss . . . albeit a highly
glamorous secretary.

As he pulled the car up alongside her, it crossed his
mind that this must be some new version of expected
kinkiness, a client waiting for her somewhere to play
office fantasies in the secret recesses of hotel bed-
rooms.

She bent down to the passenger window as George
wound it open.

'Where to?' he said.

'Can you park here?'

He looked back along the street: the car was on a
yellow line, but it was Saturday afternoon. 'I think so.'

'Come with me, then.'

'You want to *walk*?'

'The exercise will do you good.'

Sighing, George closed the window, then climbed
out of the car and locked it up. Simone was appraising
him.

'You look better in daylight,' she said.

'So do you. Where are we going?'

'Somewhere around here.'

She linked her hand into his arm as they set off along the street. Unlike previous occasions, however, her grip was light and almost affectionate.

'A bit early in the day, isn't it?' George said.

'Depends what time you start. Anyway, the early bird catches the worm.'

'The clever little bastard.'

'We go down here.'

They had arrived at the entrance to a shopping arcade, one which ran back from Piccadilly towards the lower reaches of Regent Street. The tiny shops along each side obviously pitched their wares at a wealthy clientele; the word 'exclusive' rang in George's mind. There was a watchmaker, a specialist in Wedgwood chinaware, two or three jewellers, a gown shop, a hairdresser, an importer of wines. George looked at each establishment with a kind of respectful awe, wondering what sort of job you would have to hold down to be able to buy anything here.

Simone led him to the door of what George would call a clothes shop, but which described itself, in delicate gilt lettering on a glass panel, as an outfitters. Riding gear and hunting jackets were on show in the window, together with an assortment of shooting sticks.

'These people friends of yours?' George said.

'Yes. Let me introduce you.'

She pushed open the door, which set off an old-fashioned bell attached to a spring mount. The shop smelled of leather and expensive wool. George had a bizarre image of the coming night: he and Simone driving around from one appointment to the next, she wearing hunting pink and riding cap, a leather crop in her hand. He, waiting outside, would see shadows on curtains: a man kneeling with the helmeted Simone on his back, thrashing his backside with the crop.

He had been wondering where she bought all her work clothes.

The places where George usually bought his own clothes were the sort where disco music shattered your eardrums, and persistent yobs followed your every step, waiting to pounce. This outfitters provided a hint of Mozart in the background, and the only possible assistant – a young man wearing one of the best tailored suits George had ever seen, and waiting discreetly at the rear of the shop – tactfully ignored them.

'Hold these for a moment,' Simone said, handing him a selection of men's ties.

'Thanks.'

He followed her through the shop, curious to see what she would buy. Her next choice was some shirts, wrapped up in crisp cellophane bags.

'A couple of these, I think.'

'You like men's clothes?' George said.

'They're sometimes necessary.' She had come to a rack of suits, and started to sift through them. 'How about a thin stripe?'

'It's classy.'

'A herringbone, I think. You can't tell whether it's a stripe or not.'

'Yeah . . . that one looks good.'

Simone unhooked it from the rack, held it up to look at, then laid it against George's chest.

'Lovely,' she said. 'What do you think?'

George took it from her, and held it against her.

'You'd have to do something about your tits.'

She grinned. 'No, it's for you.'

'For *me*?'

'Yes . . . who do you think?'

'I thought it was for you.'

'Go and try it on,' she said.

George frowned, and moved to return the suit to the rack. 'You can't go around dressing me.'

'Yes I can. Try it on.'

'No.'

'George, if you're working with me you've got to dress up right.'

'I said *no*.'

She lowered her voice. 'Take the fucking thing, would you? We're being looked at.'

The assistant had been staring in their direction, but as soon as George turned his head he looked away.

'Are you serious?' George said.

'Please.'

'Might as well then, eh?'

'Yes, you might as well,' she said, sounding resigned.

That night, wearing his new clothes, George parked the Jaguar in the car park outside the hotel in Cumberland Gate. It had taken him a while, but when all was said and done the new clothes made him feel better about the entire business.

It started in the outfitters: the suit had had to be fitted to him, and the elegant young assistant had offered to make the alterations on the spot. The curiously intimate process of having measurements taken, while Simone watched straightfaced, followed by the changing into and out of his old clothes while the new suit was altered, had made him feel much closer to Simone and more relaxed with her.

They had gone their separate ways in the afternoon, and now here they were, back again in the business.

As he switched off the engine, George was finishing a story he was telling her.

'. . . so there was this frog . . .' he said.

'We're late.'

Simone opened the car door, and swung her legs out. Gone was the stunning secretarial look of the day, and now she was back in her grey overcoat. As she moved, George was afforded a ravishing glimpse of long black thighs. He wondered what the rest of the concealed costume looked like this evening.

He scrambled to follow her, then took her arm.

'. . . and no one wanted to kiss him,' he went on.

They passed the commissionaire, and swung through the revolving door.

'Why not?' Simone said.

'You know the way frogs are. All sticky. So, one day, he –'

Simone turned to face him, and gave him the briefest of kisses on his cheek.

'Yeah, I know,' she said.

'You know the story?'

'Turning into a prince.'

'Well there's this twist, see –'

'You'll have to save it for later. I've got work to do.'

With that she turned and walked up the stairs. Again there was the stunning combination of grace and speed. She moved clutching the coat modestly around her, with not a hint of what she was, what she was about to do.

The waiter with the pigtail was watching him. George started to go up to him, thought better of it, and went to find a table.

'The usual, sir?'

'Usual? How many times have I been here?'

'Bloody Mary, isn't it? With?'

'Yeah, that's right . . . the usual.'

But he felt more at home here now. It was the clothes that did it. Maybe they just looked better, or maybe it was the knowledge that for once in his life he had real class, and this gave him confidence . . . but he no longer felt like a spare prick at a party.

He had taken two sips of his drink, and was glancing up the grand staircase, prematurely looking for Simone, when he noticed that one of the function rooms on the upper floor was in use. The double doors stood open, and a member of the hotel staff, dressed impeccably in an evening suit, was standing there checking the invitations of all those who went in.

Many people were moving about on the landing, some of them having spilled out from the party inside, others heading for the doors.

One of them was Mortwell.

Abandoning his drink, George went quickly across

the lobby and took the stairs two at a time. He headed straight for the doors. Mortwell had already gone inside.

'And your invitation, sir?'

It was the man in the evening suit, gently blocking his way. But firmly, ever so firmly.

'I just want to talk to someone,' George said, trying to see past the man into the throng within.

'Yes, sir. If I could just see your invitation?'

George glimpsed Mortwell inside.

'Dinny!' he shouted. '*Dinny!*'

He forced his way past the man at the door, and shouted Mortwell's name again. Behind him, the man was tugging at the jacket of his new suit.

At that moment Mortwell turned, and saw George. He immediately broke off from his conversation, and pushed across to him.

'Jesus Christ, George!'

With Mortwell shoving him and the hotel man pulling, George was outside on the landing in seconds. He grinned at Mortwell.

'What am I doing here, right?' he said.

'I didn't say that.'

'OK. But here I am.'

'Great to see you again, George, great.' Mortwell was already backing away from him.

'Dinny, listen –'

'I'm a bit tied up at the moment, but –'

'No, I got to talk to you!'

While he was trying to get his word in edgeways, George was aware that someone was hovering behind Mortwell, obviously waiting to speak to him. Mortwell knew he was there.

'I'll call you, George.'

'Leave it out, Dinny. You never call anyone.'

Mortwell looked back at the man standing behind him, and George, for the first time, realised who it was. The last time he had seen that little pointed beard was – The tray, the sandwiches, the house in St John's Wood.

Mortwell turned his back on George, spoke swiftly and sincerely to the Arab, who smiled his agreement and walked calmly through the doors into the main party. No one asked to see his invitation.

Mortwell said: 'Come on, George, you can see I'm busy.'

'Yeah, I'm sorry. But listen, I've been trying to contact you.'

'I thought Dudley had looked after you.'

'He did, but – Nothing like the personal touch, is there? Seven years, Dinny. . .'

'This isn't the time.'

'We've a lot to talk about,' George said.

'So we have. I'll ring you as soon as I can.'

'Is that a promise?'

'Would I let you down?' He winked broadly at George, and raised a hand, a mocking wave. George did the same. Each mocked the other. Dinny never phoned anyone.

'We've got to talk.'

'I've promised, George . . .'

Then he was gone. George stared after him, through the doors and into the milling crowd of people, knowing Mortwell had always tried to take him for a mug.

* * *

Two Bloody Marys later, George's spirits had revived a little. When Simone reappeared he stood up at once and offered her his arm. She linked her hand through, pressed herself against him, and they walked out together to the car park.

'Good?' George said.

'What do you mean?'

'You know what I mean! Was it good?'

She made an exasperated noise.

'George . . . what's *wrong* with you?'

'I dunno. What is wrong with me?'

At the end of the long night, with half a dozen calls behind them, George and Simone were back on the bridge at King's Cross. She was in the rear passenger seat, crouching low so she could hardly be seen, and staring out at the low trade in progress.

'You like this place, don't you?' George said.

'No.'

'You seem to.'

'I hate it, if you must know.'

George stared forward, watching the girls patrolling the kerbside.

'See that one there,' he said. 'I've got a daughter her age.'

'They're all daughters to somebody. It's just that yours isn't one of them.'

'Christ, I hope not,' George said.

The one he had pointed out was looking towards him, and now she left her place and came directly towards the car.

'She's coming over,' George said. 'You want to leave?'

Simone said nothing, locked in her fascinated watching of the street.

The young prostitute came up to the window of the car. She bent down, her loose blouse hanging forward to reveal most of her tiny breasts.

'You want to do it?' she said. She was chewing on some gum.

'Nah . . . it's all right, thank you.' He stared ahead, feeling embarrassed with Simone sitting back there in the shadows.

'I'm good, darlin',' the girl said. 'I'm very good indeed. I do french, and I do twosomes.'

'Go home, luv, will you?'

'What's the matter with you?' She was turning suddenly aggressive. She tried to open the car door, but George, with unusual foresight, had locked it on the inside. Still bending low to the window, the prostitute said: 'I know your type, you cunt! You want to look, and you want to have it . . . but you won't pay for it, will you?' She brought her face closer. 'Here . . . I've seen you before, haven't I?'

She was pushed aside by the arrival of a man: not another punter, but the pimp who ran her life.

'He at you, Rosie?' he said, thrusting her into the background. He crouched down so that his face was level with George's. George continued to stare straight ahead, wishing he was anywhere else in London apart from here.

'If you don't want her, squire, you go fuck your-self. Fuck off out of here, and take your fucking car with you.'

George had a rooted objection to being talked to like this, and he turned to face the pimp. He was a nasty-looking young man in flashy clothes. He had the sort of face it was impossible to kick only once.

'You hear what I say,' the pimp said. He looked in the back of the car, and at last saw Simone, huddling there. 'You! What the fuck are you doing here?'

'George, get driving!'

But George was angry, and the words didn't register.

The pimp said to Simone: 'If Anderson finds you he's going to cut your face up. You hear?'

'Drive!'

'You nigger tom, nigger tom!'

'Mind your fucking language!' shouted George. It suddenly burst in him, and he reached through the open window, grabbed the pimp's head and crashed his jaw down on the metal sill of the window. There was a cracking sound, so George did it again. Harder. He got a fist free, and smashed the man in the face.

'Now look what you made me do!' he said, as the man reeled back, and sprawled on the ground.

Simone screamed from the back. 'I said, get the fuck *out* of here!'

At last George was ready. As the pimp struggled to get to his feet, George wound the window up, shoved the car into gear and accelerated away. Two prostitutes, crossing the road, had to scurry out of the way.

He didn't slow the car until they were in the Caledonian Road, and then, driving more steadily, but still breathing heavily, he said: 'Jesus H.'

Simone was somewhere in the back. He turned his head to look, and she was sprawled across the seat, as shaken by the encounter as he was.

'I thought you were high class and respectable,' he said.

'Whatever gave you that idea?'

'I dunno. I always seem to get things wrong.'

Chapter 10

George brought the car to a halt outside Simone's block of flats, and switched off the engine. His right hand was hurting, so he switched on the interior light and examined it. A bruised gash had appeared on the heel of his hand, and blood had seeped into the cuff of his new shirt and jacket.

'Look at that,' he said, with some pride. 'I wonder how the pimp's feeling?'

'I don't want to find out,' Simone said from the back.

'Are you going to tell me what all that was about?'

'Do you have to know?'

'If I'm going to go on driving you around.'

There was a short silence. Then: 'All right, but not here. Come inside for a few minutes.'

'You sure?'

But she was already out of the car and walking towards the main entrance. George locked up and followed her.

The main door was protected by a double lock and an entry phone, and the hall inside was bare and tiled. It led to a corridor branching off in opposite directions, and a lift with a mesh gate. Concrete stairs spiralled around the lift shaft. Simone punched the button for the ninth floor.

An upwards lurch, and a distant whining. George watched the landings slide down and past. Someone, a long time ago, had painted the number of each floor on the concrete sill as the lift approached that level, and he counted them off to himself, one by one.

Simone's flat was at the far end of one of the corridors, and it too was protected by a double lock. She led him into her living room, which felt pleasantly warm. It was decorated tastefully; the room gave the impression that she had lived here a long time, that she liked the place, and that she had spent a good deal of money on furnishing it properly.

She put down her bag, then opened one of the windows to let in some fresh air.

'Let me look at your hand,' she said, and George obligingly held it out towards her. She turned it over gingerly, looked at both sides.

'Where did you learn to do all that?' she said.

'I picked it up. You know –'

'On the way. Sit down there, and I'll clean you up.'

She went towards a connecting door, removing her grey overcoat as she walked. Just as she vanished into the next room, George caught a glimpse of what she had been wearing underneath: the tiniest of miniskirts, and a wisp of transparent blouse. She closed the door on him, and when she returned a minute or so later she was wearing an oriental robe. She had loosened her hair.

Simone went through to the kitchen, and came back a moment later with a bowl of warm water, a wad of cotton wool and a small sponge.

'OK,' she said. 'This –'

'I know . . . it's going to hurt.'

'It'll sting slightly.'

71

She dabbed gently at his hand and cleaned out the graze. Then, using the sponge, she dabbed at the bloodstains on his clothes. They weren't very extensive, but both she and George felt respectful of his new outfit.

'How come you know little shits like that?' George said.

'The pimp?'

'Yeah.'

'Just like you. I pick these things up as I go along.'

She set aside the sponge and the bowl of water.

'What about Anderson? Who's that?'

'Another pimp. A ponce.'

'Yours?' said George.

'He's an animal . . . born in a butcher's shop.'

'But do you have a ponce?'

'No.' Simone settled down on the rug in front of him, sitting cross-legged with the robe arranged over her legs. 'I don't need one. I've got you to protect me.'

'This Anderson,' said George. 'He used to knock you about?'

'He used to adjust my face . . . yes.'

'Why didn't you leave?'

'He told me he'd cut me up. Then he told me I was wonderful.'

'All in the same breath.'

'That's what a good ponce does,' said Simone. 'He drives flash cars and wears gold jewellery . . . and lives in a room with a paraffin heater.'

'But why didn't you get out?'

Simone shifted position, looking uncomfortable.

'You don't know very much, do you, George? You

don't know what it's like.' But the familiar accusation came this time without bitterness. Simone was staring at the carpet. 'Anyway, I had a friend then. He ran the both of us. She was much younger than me. Beautiful, and white. She had a habit, was in a lot of trouble. That's why I stayed.'

'You could've both got out.'

'Do you know what a habit is?'

'She bit her nails . . . like me.'

Anger flickered momentarily in Simone's eyes, but then vanished.

'This was the sort of habit that involved sticking needles in her arm. Anderson supplied her with the shit. Let's have a drink . . . I need one.' She got up quickly, and went to a cabinet at the side of the room. When she returned she held two glasses of neat Scotch. 'Well, one day I couldn't take it any more. I met a man with a gold ring who took me to Brighton. We were in one of those hotels along the front, the one that was blown up. When I woke up in the morning he was gone. But I didn't mind. He'd already paid me, and I could see the sea outside. I went on the beach, then walked along the pier. I met another man there, and that paid the hotel bill for another night. I sat in the tea room at the Grand, and met another. I began to see how things could be different, so I stayed the whole summer. I saved a lot of money. Anderson couldn't find me. At the end of the season I came back to London and found this place. I learned about the West End hotels, and how to do business in them. It was a different world. I started looking for Cathy, but I've never seen her since. She used to work that street in King's Cross.'

She reached behind her, and found a photograph album lying on the floor under a chair. The album fell open easily in one place: two pages of Polaroid pictures.

'Look,' said Simone, turning the album around and giving it to George. 'This is Cathy. She's a Londoner.'

She was young-looking and frail, with thin features and straw-coloured hair. But she had the unconscious radiance that gives beauty, and although in the pictures she was wrapped up in a thick anorak and a woollen hat, George could see that she had the same natural elegance as Simone, the same self-assurance of body.

'She has a tattoo on her right hand,' Simone said. 'Like this.' She described a small heart with her fingertip, across the back of her hand. 'Tiny and blue, with a smaller one inside.'

George stared at the pictures of the girl, thinking again of youth and vice and his daughter, and how narrow a line it was that could be crossed, how vulnerable some teenage girls could be.

'I don't know her,' he said, not knowing what sort of response Simone was expecting.

'I promised I'd look after her,' Simone said. 'Anything can happen out there . . . on the streets, in the clubs. I'd pay you.'

'What for?'

'I can't go down there. But you could. I'd give you anything you ask.'

'What . . . money?'

'I'll pay any way I can. I have to find her. You know the way it is.'

'Yeah,' said George.

'You're a good man, Mr George.'

'How can you tell?'

'I can. Will you think about it?'

'All right.'

'You promise?'

'Yeah . . . 'course I promise. You want me just to find her. That all?'

'No more than that.' She took the album from him, and closed it. 'Now it's time for me to go to bed. Goodnight, George.'

'Can I finish my drink first?'

She smiled, and when he put down his empty glass she led him to the door.

On his way back to Thomas' place, George took a detour and drove through the King's Cross area again. He went with some caution across the bridge, imagining the pimp still lurking there, waiting with a gang to exact some nameless revenge on him. But it was late now, and most of the girls had left. He saw two prostitutes still on patrol, standing together in the cone of amber light beneath a lamppost, and as his headlights picked them out they both looked up expectantly. As he swept past it seemed to him that their pallid faces were like those of drowning swimmers, sinking in an ocean of corruption.

Chapter 11

He thought Thomas was asleep, but as he moved around in the cramped confines of the caravan, sliding out of his new clothes, the lumpen shape on the other bunk stirred.

'George?'

'Nnn,' he said, non-committally.

More movement, and the caravan shook on its unsteady mounts. There was the pop of a match, and the hiss of a propane gas mantle. Yellow light shone out uncertainly. Thomas was sitting up; he was wearing a check shirt.

'G'night, Thomas,' George said.

'I wanted to ask you something.'

'Is it important?'

'It is to me. Have you got to the bit where the dwarf loses his memory for the third time?'

'I thought you were asleep.'

'No. Well, have you?'

'I haven't been getting much time for reading lately. She keeps me busy.'

Thomas peered at George's neat pile of clothes.

'So did she like them?'

'She *bought* them, didn't she?'

'I suppose she did. Sorry.'

'Goodnight, Thomas.'

George climbed into his own bunk, and tried to make himself comfortable. Thomas sat there a while longer with the light on, but in the end he reached up and turned it off.

In spite of being dog-tired, George found sleep slow to arrive. His hand was hurting, and his mind was turning.

In the end, he said into the darkness: 'I got to find a girl, Thomas.'

'Thought you already had.'

'Nah, not her. Somebody else.'

'I knew it'd never work out.'

'Listen, it's a sort of favour. It's a girl gone missing. She's young, on the game. I know what she looks like, well sort of, but she could be anywhere.'

'Ask around.'

'What . . . go up to people in the street? "I'm looking for a whore"?'

'That's one way of going about it. Depends what street you're in.'

George thought for a while.

'But suppose she's got out, doing something else? She could be anywhere in London.'

'Ask around, George.'

'Yeah . . . maybe I will.'

He had a consignment of video tapes to bring in from St Albans, and it took him most of the Monday morning. In the afternoon, with an hour or two to kill, George parked his car at a meter in Soho Square and went for a walk.

He headed down Greek Street, then turned off into one of the numerous back lanes and alleys that led off

77

into the seedier areas. He went into the first place he found, on the principle he had to begin somewhere.

There were two men standing at the door, and as soon as he approached they shifted position, ready for him.

'You got girls in here?' George said.

'What you think?' one of the men said, in a heavy foreign accent. There was a crudely lettered sign behind him saying TOPLESS BAR, and GORGEOUS HOSTESSES. Underneath was a picture of a nude woman. She was sitting on a stool holding a beach ball. The picture looked as if it had been taken in 1950.

'OK,' said George, and made to go in. The other man immediately caught his arm.

'Three pounds.'

'Three quid, just to walk through a door?'

'It's a club. You gotta join.'

Muttering under his breath, George dug a fiver out of his pocket and handed it over. In return he was given a pink cloakroom ticket with a number on it.

He shouldered his way past the men, and went down unsteady wooden stairs into the cellar.

The bar surprised him mildly: the Paradise Club had prepared him for another dump, but this place revealed what was at least a minimal effort at providing decor. The tables had cloths on them, there were velvet hangings against the wall and heavy Tiffany lampshades lent a certain atmosphere. But the place smelt damp.

He was the only customer. Three or four girls sat in a group at one of the tables, and as he walked in they perked up and looked his way.

George ignored them, and went to the bar. A young woman with a mass of flame-red hair was wiping up glasses.

He looked pointedly at her chest and said: 'I thought this was a topless bar.'

'After six o'clock. Regulations.'

'You should say that on the door.'

'Uh-huh, you want a drink?'

She had heard it all before. George had a glimpse of this woman's working day: men coming in and demanding to see her tits, then at six in the evening she would resignedly peel off her T-shirt, and the men would pretend not to look.

'I said, you want a drink?'

'No thanks.'

'You buy a ticket, then you buy a drink. Those are the rules.'

'How much?'

'Five pounds minimum.'

'On top of the three to get in?'

'I don't make the rules. You want to meet a girl, you have to buy a drink.'

George glanced back at the table. There were no blondes there.

'Look . . . before I buy a drink, will you tell me something?'

'What?'

'You got any blonde girls here?'

The girl smiled, unexpectedly.

'Sure we have.'

She reached up, and pulled at her hair. The red wig came away, revealing a boyish, elfin head, blonde hair, close-cropped. In that moment she was transformed.

'What do you think?' she said, still grinning at him.

George found a strip club further down the same alley, forked out ten pounds and went down into yet another cellar. As he went in a woman wearing a Nazi helmet, jackboots and nothing else was striding to and fro on a tiny platform, accompanied by heavily distorted disco music. An audience of five or six men were watching; each was seated alone, away from the others.

George stood at the back for a minute or two, then noticed a door marked 'No Entry'. No one said anything as he opened it, so he squeezed his way along a narrow corridor. The music, if anything, was louder here.

He came to a small alcove. It was crammed with costumes, but a girl was crouching in the space on the floor. At first all he could see of her was a naked back, with pimples all over her shoulder blades, but when she heard him and turned he saw she was wearing a faded purple leotard.

She said: 'Who the fuck are you?'

Because she had moved, George could now see what she had been doing on the floor. There was a tiny primus stove with a kettle, and next to it a teapot and some mugs.

'Here,' he said, grinning at her. 'Any chance of a cup of tea?'

'Piss off, punter.'

'Don't be like that . . . I didn't get any lunch.'

'How the hell did you get in here?'

'All right, I'm sorry. Sorry I asked.'

He backed away. The alcove was set into the wall at

the corner of the narrow corridor, and looking further along he could see through to the tiny stage. The woman in the Nazi helmet had finished her act, and had been replaced by a tiny Japanese girl. She, stark naked and crouching obscenely with her backside towards the audience, was doing something interesting with a piece of rope.

Behind him, the girl in the leotard said: 'If you don't piss off straight away, I'll call the boys in.'

'I've gone, darlin'. Cheerio.'

George decided to pursue his quest elsewhere.

There was a peep show in the same building as one of his drops for video tapes, and because he was beginning to feel discouraged George thought he would try somewhere that felt remotely familiar.

Peep shows were new to him; they must have sprung into existence while he was inside. He entered the door with a feeling of curiosity.

A gloomy corridor, painted black, led to a glassed-in desk, and here a resentful punk girl, with hair spiking into vermilion points, changed notes into 50p coins.

'It's OK,' George said. 'I've got a pocketful of them.'

'You have to change them here. Rules.'

'All right . . . how much?'

'Minimum of five pounds.'

George handed over a fiver, and was given nine coins in return.

'And the rest,' he said.

'That's the membership fee.'

'Those rules . . . they don't say anything about six o'clock, do they?'

The girl gaped at him, so he went on through. Immediately beyond the next door was the peep show itself: a group of curtained booths clustered around the metal box inside which the women performed.

George found an empty booth, and slipped a coin into the slot. A metal shutter flipped open, just below comfortable eye level, and he leaned forward to see what was going on.

The interior of the peep show was lit by two bare lightbulbs. A transistor radio sat on the floor, squawking out pop music. Two naked girls gyrated with bored expressions, performing to the circle of slits in the metal walls that surrounded them. Most of them were open, with hungry eyes visible behind, but some of the shutters were sliding relentlessly down as the money ran out.

George's arrival provoked the only sign of interest in the two women: one of them moved over to his shutter, shook her breasts a couple of times, then raised a leg to give him a close-up view.

With a grinding noise, his shutter began to close.

George reached instinctively for another coin, then shook his head in dismay and decided he had better things to do with his time.

He backed out of the cubicle; as the light from the corridor fell briefly into it he noticed that the floor was littered with pieces of screwed-up newspaper.

Around the back of the peep show box there was a door with PRIVATE written on it in chalk, so George opened it and walked in. Immediately beyond was a beaded curtain. He went in. Four girls sat in the squalid, smoke-filled room. They were waiting their turn, wearing robes and housecoats and garish make-up. None of them looked up.

One said: 'Get the fuck out, whoever you are.'

'I'm not a punter,' George said, raising the palms of his hands as if in disclaimer. 'I'm looking for someone.'

The girl nearest him put down her newspaper.

'How many times a day do you suppose we hear shit like that? Get out.'

'Her name's Cathy, she's got blonde hair and a blue tattoo on one hand.'

'Call Directory Enquiries.'

'Stick 50p in the slot, John,' said another.

'Just asking,' said George, hating all this.

'You asked, we answered. Now piss off, will you?'

Feeling humiliated, George backed out of the room. He returned to the main area, where the cubicles were, and saw that in the few moments since he had been there someone had wheeled in a pressure-pump and was squirting spray on the walls. As George closed the door behind him, liquid splashed over him. He ducked, and raised an arm.

'Here! Watch out!'

'Don't worry, guv, it's only disinfectant.' The man with the spray lowered the nozzle. 'Christ! It's you, George! Didn't know you were into all this.'

It was Terry.

'I've had seven years inside. What's your excuse?'

'It's a living. Well, what's your fancy?'

'You arrange things, Terry?'

'Can do. What you want?'

'I'll tell you exactly. I met a young kid once, on the game. Nice girl called Cathy.'

'And?'

'She used to work in a club around here, but I forget which one she said it was.'

'What's she look like?'

'Spiky hair, a blonde. Not spiky like the bird out there on the desk, but sort of cut short on top.'

Terry stared at him with a thoughtful expression.

'You know you might be in luck, George.'

'Do you know who I mean? Got a tattoo.'

'On her bum, isn't it?'

'On the back of her hand. Two hearts, one inside the other.'

Terry looked interested. 'Come back here in an hour, George.'

'Can't, not then. I gotta work.'

'Later, then. Come this evening.'

George thought about it, knowing there were long gaps in the night when all he had to do was sit in a car.

'All right. Here?'

'No . . . the Go-Go. See what I can do. I'll be there.'

'Any time?'

'Any time you like, George.'

Chapter 12

It was raining that night, and as George drove Simone through the West End to her first appointment he felt the weather adequately summed up his own depressing state of mind. He wished he had the same cynical attitude as Terry: a job, a living, something to do to have money in your pocket. Well, he was earning a crust, but there was all the other stuff too.

He said to Simone: 'Don't it make you sick?'

'What?'

'The business.'

'What about you? Does it make you sick?'

'Yeah,' George said. 'But I'm not in it, am I?'

'Aren't you?' Simone laughed, making George look at her. 'You're in it, all right. Deep in it.'

This made him feel even gloomier, and he shut up, thinking how quickly he had leapt to the judgement about people crossing lines, and all that. He was driving slowly and pedantically this evening, like a reluctant child dragging his way to school.

They arrived at the hotel in Cumberland Gate, and parked.

'Those places cost real money, you know,' he said.

'Is that what's making you sick?'

'Part of it.'

'Take it from the float. I can afford it, and you're doing it for me.'

'Yeah, but –'

They were walking across the concourse towards the commissionaire by the main doors. When they were a few feet away, they both noticed that someone who had been standing inside the lobby, looking out through the glass doors, had moved back.

Simone quickly took George's arm.

'That was the house detective. He's on to me.'

'What can he do?'

'Oh . . . not much. Have me arrested, thrown in jail. Not a lot.'

'You want to go on in?'

'I've got to. Listen . . . tonight, stay by me. OK? Come up with me.'

'Just like a regular couple.'

'Yes, dearest.'

The commissionaire nodded to them politely, and even swung the door into motion for them. George let Simone go first, then followed. Inside, she took his arm again and kissed him affectionately on the cheek.

They walked through the lobby, pretending to be wrapped up in each other.

Waiting for the lift to arrive, George whispered: 'He's jealous.'

'That's one way of looking at it.'

When the lift doors had closed on them they unlinked arms, and Simone made hasty adjustments to her hair.

'What next?' George said. 'Want me to come in with you, lend a hand?'

'Don't get ideas. You're just my driver, OK?'

'I don't understand you, Simone.'

'You're not meant to.'

The lift came to a halt and the doors opened automatically. The hotel passageway stretched away on either side, deserted and opulent. George followed her out.

'That's it, George. You leave me here.'

'What do you want me to do? Wait downstairs?'

'Whatever you like. Just be there when I'm ready.'

'How long are you going to be?'

'This call? An hour, maybe an hour and a half.'

'I'll be in the lounge.'

She turned away from him.

'Wait!' he said, and she paused. 'Your hair . . . you messed it up just then.' He reached up and smoothed down a rough patch. 'We have to look our best, don't we?'

'You're getting very considerate all of a sudden.'

'Yeah, I know,' he said. 'I'm like that. Cheap . . . but considerate.'

He left the car at the hotel and took a cab to Soho. He had said nothing to Simone about Terry's promise, and wanted to surprise her. At the same time, though, he knew she'd probably kill him if he wasn't waiting in the lobby for her. He had to be back within the hour, just to be sure.

The Go-Go Club was in a narrow lane behind Dean Street, reached by way of a rickety staircase. George pushed his way past the bouncers on the door, unwilling to go through the rigmarole of rules and membership and the rest of the scam. They seemed indifferent to him, and after the token threats and abuse had followed him up the stairs they turned back to their normal business of hassling passers-by.

Rather to George's surprise Terry was actually there, sitting in his ludicrous suit with a group of hostesses. When George walked in he left them at once, and came over.

'Well?' said George. 'What about it?'

'I did my best.'

'And?'

'I'm surprised at you, George.'

'Why's that?'

'She's young, very young.'

'Well, you know the way it is . . . But is she the right one?'

'Cathy . . . her name's Cathy. Tattoo and everything. Look, I'm tied up at the moment. Tim will take you to her.'

'Who the hell's Tim?'

'Wait here.'

Terry went out of the door, and came back a few moments later with one of the bouncers from outside. The man jerked his head, indicating that George should follow him. Without saying anything he led him up two more flights of stairs, then pointed to a door.

'You got twenty minutes.'

'All right, all right. I can tell the time.'

'Don't mess the goods up, man.'

George gave him a contemptuous look, and went into the room.

Chapter 13

There was a girl lying on a bed, and the bed occupied much of the dingy room. There was only one light on: a small table lamp next to the bed. The shade was, of course, red, but it was plastic and faded. It lent pathos and cheapness to the room, not sultry promise of passion.

George stood by the door, still resting his fingers on the handle, as if in need of a hurried escape.

The girl smiled up at him as soon as he had closed the door, and it was a brittle, earnest smile, devoid of pleasure or even expertise.

'Hello,' she said. 'Come on in.'

'Are you Cathy?' George said.

'That's right, I'm Cathy. What's your name?'

'George.'

'Well, come and sit beside me, George.' She patted the bed beside her.

The words came out of her in a practised, formulaic flow, like lines learnt by a child. After some hesitation, George went and sat on the side of the bed, where she had indicated, but as he did so he saw that the childlike quality was not assumed. If she was older than fifteen, he was a Dutchman. She had the unformed physique of an adolescent: the unrounded body that had only recently stopped growing, the direct eyes that lacked deviousness, the slim hips and small breasts of immaturity.

Yet she was dolled up like a whore, like a predatory slut: a tiny, tight skirt, showing a hint of exotic suspenders, a transparent blouse, a token black bra all too visible beneath.

And now he was close to her he could see that her face bore marks: dark bruises, ill-concealed beneath a cake of make-up.

'Where are you from, Cathy?' he said, feeling paternal.

'I'm from here.'

She bent forward unexpectedly, thrusting her mouth down on his knees then moving quickly up until her head was in his lap. As he felt her lips working on him through the fabric of his clothes George moved her head away with his hand, and turned his body so that she could not do it again.

'Don't do that,' he said.

'You've got to tell me what you want, so I can please you.'

'I want to *talk*.'

'Ssh!' She pointed towards the door. 'The walls are thin here, and he's out there listening. He'll be angry if you don't come out happy.'

'I am happy.' The words sounded flat and unconvincing, even to him.

'He thinks I'm no good. But I am good, aren't I?'

'You are good.'

'It doesn't mean you can't talk.'

'Where did you get the bruises, Cathy?'

She looked away sharply. 'My name's May.'

'Let me see.' He grabbed her right hand, and

looked at it in the light. Two crude hearts had been drawn on her hand with a blue ballpoint. 'Who did this?'

'He did . . . he said it was what you wanted.'

'Yeah . . . well, not that way. Was it him who bruised you?'

'He gets angry.'

He knew now for certain that she was not the girl he was seeking. Even her accent was not from London.

He said: 'Where do you come from, May?'

'Bradford.'

'Oh, Christ.'

'What?'

'I wanted someone else . . . the real Cathy.'

She lowered her voice, trying to make it sultry. 'Don't say that, George. Don't say that.'

'You mean he'll hit you again?'

'Yes.'

She lunged towards his lap again, and he had to move her forcibly away. Holding her head in both hands he said: 'Listen to me, May. He's not going to hit you.'

'Not if you're happy.'

'I *am* happy. I told you.'

She looked as if she were about to cry.

'Tell him that . . . for God's sake tell him that I made you happy.'

'I will.'

'Promise me, George.'

'I promise. But I gotta go now, see. Just don't be frightened.'

He released his hands, and stood up slowly, backing

away. She didn't move again, a huddled, frightened child, about to cry, about to be beaten again for something she hadn't done. That he had not let her do.

Feeling ashamed, but also helpless, George let himself out of the room and closed the door behind him.

He stood in the corridor for a moment, shaking his head, wondering at his own stupidity and clumsiness. There must be a better way than this –

Someone was standing there, in the shadows. He moved towards George.

'Happy?' he said.

George turned in surprise.

'Yes . . . Yes, I'm happy.'

'She make you feel good?'

George shook his head again, this time simulating awe. 'My God, she knows what she's doin'!'

'Forty-eight.'

The man was a tall, muscular black, dressed in a smart suit. He seemed to fill the narrow passageway, and stood over George by at least twelve inches.

George took out some money, and counted forty-eight pounds into the man's hand.

'She's a good girl, Cathy. One of my best.'

'Very good. The top.'

'Come back any time you like. She'll be here.'

'I will, I promise. I can't wait for the next time.'

'Just ask for me.'

'What's your name, Mr . . .?'

'Smith. Mr Smith.'

Smith walked with George to the head of the stairs, his arm around his shoulders in a fraternal way. But he did not follow him down the stairs, and as George reached the next landing below he heard fast-moving footsteps on the bare boards, followed by the sound of a door being opened.

Chapter 14

For some reason it took him a while to find a taxi, and by the time he was back at the hotel in Cumberland Gate George knew he was cutting it fine. He entered the hotel lobby feeling anxious, anticipating Simone's violent fury if he had let her down.

Preoccupied with her, he didn't notice the hotel detective, who walked quickly over and tapped him on the shoulder.

'Hotel security,' the man said.

'Yeah . . . what does that mean?'

'It means you've brought a tom into the hotel.'

'A what?' said George.

'A tom. A tart.'

'I've no idea what you're talking about. I'm here with my wife.'

'Look, I've seen you. I know what you're up to. Where's your . . . wife now?'

'She's visiting friends.'

'And what might be the number of their room?'

'That's none of your damned business.' With a feeling of tremendous relief, George saw Simone leaving the lift, and waved to her. She hurried over, a smile wreathed on her face. 'Ready darling?' George said.

Simone kissed him warmly.

'Sorry to keep you waiting, George. We had so much to talk about!'

The detective had been watching this sceptically, and as George and Simone walked arm in arm towards the door he prodded George on the shoulder.

'You! I'm warning you . . . next time.'

George turned on him in simulated rage.

'Who the *hell* are you talking to?' he roared. 'Me or my wife?'

The detective visibly wilted, and they walked quickly on. Just as they approached the revolving door, Simone said loudly: 'Darling, who was that awful little man you were talking to?'

They got to the car, and closed the doors. The detective had followed them outside, and was now standing on the hotel steps. He had a little notepad, and was writing something in it . . . presumably the car's licence plate number.

'He's on to you,' George said.

'He's been on to me for weeks. Let's go, I'm late again.'

George started the car and they began the short drive to her next appointment.

'So what does he want?'

'A slice of the action . . . just like a ponce.'

'You mean they're fucking everywhere. They're all on the game.'

'Haven't you noticed?'

At the end of the night, as they drove back towards Simone's place, George said: 'I've been to more clubs, looking around.'

'And?'

'I'm not having a good time.'

'You're not supposed to. Are you getting anywhere?'

'Well . . . I didn't tell you, but this evening while you were on one of your calls I went to see someone. I met a girl. She was about fifteen and she had bruises on her face. She said she wanted to make me happy.'

'What was her name?'

'It wasn't Cathy,' George said. 'The man who set it up, he said her name was Cathy, but they were taking me for a mug. It wasn't the girl you're looking for.'

'Are you sure?'

'Is the one you're looking for from Bradford? Is she about fifteen years old?'

'No. . . .'

'How old is she?'

'Older than that. Not much, though.'

They had reached Simone's street, and George found a place to park. He switched off the engine.

'Is that what you say to your clients? "I'll make you happy"?'

'Sometimes. Depends.'

'On what?'

'You know. . . some of them like to have a bad time.'

'Amounts to the same thing, I suppose.' George stared down the homely Islington street. 'My God, why am I doing all this?'

'Don't you know why?' George shook his head. 'Because I asked you to . . . and maybe because you're curious.'

Sometimes Thomas suffocated him, with his endless fanciful talk about novels. He didn't seem to realise that sitting around on your bum for several years gave the pleasures of reading a whole new edge . . . and equally, that a long working day ate into your spare time like nothing else. Spare time was when he read.

Unexpectedly he had an afternoon off, and, with what developed into fine irony, had planned to catch up on some of the novels Thomas kept thrusting at him. Instead, Thomas wanted to talk about the same books, and after an hour of this George went out for a drive on his own.

Around four o'clock, he was in the Wandsworth sidestreet, watching the kids leave school. He hadn't planned this, and had no idea what he thought would happen, but there he was, looking for Jeanie.

She came out late, walking with two friends, arms linked, but not looking particularly happy. George stared at her, wondering how to bridge the abyss that had opened between them.

She was about to pass him, unnoticing, when a sideways glance met his eyes. She looked surprised, but instantly unlinked arms and came to a halt. Her friends went on a few paces, then stopped to wait for her.

She came to the passenger window, and George leaned over to wind it down.

'Is this your car, Dad?'

'Yeah. Do you like it?'

'It's nice.'

'I clean it every day.'

'Can I get in?'

' 'Course you can.' He pushed it open for her, and after a smile to her friends Jeanie climbed in beside him. The girls giggled, and went off down the road.

'They're jealous,' she said, with some satisfaction.

'Good friends of yours?'

'Sort of.'

She settled back in the old leather seat, wriggling luxuriously. Then she sat forward to look at the radio, the tape player. George pressed a knob on the dash, and made the aerial go up and down automatically.

'Want a lift home?' he said.

'All right.'

'I'll go the long way round. So we can talk a bit.'

After another inspection of the inside of the car, Jeanie said: 'You made a right mess that day.'

'I know. I'm sorry.'

'So you should be.'

'What did your mother say afterwards?'

'Nothing. She never talks about you.'

'That so, eh? Never?'

'Why did you go away and leave her?'

'Didn't she tell you?'

'No.'

That was news to him. 'Then I won't, either,' he said.

'Go on, I want to know.'

'I'm a bad lot, Jeanie. I'll tell you some day.'

'Are you still a bad lot?'

'Not for me to say, is it?'

They got into a traffic hold-up near Wandsworth Town Hall, but once they were through the one-way system they soon came to the corner of Jeanie's street. He had gone a long way round, but the school was, after all, only within walking distance.

He pulled over to the side.

'You'd better go now,' he said.

'Will you pick me up from school again?'

'Your mother wouldn't like it.'

'I can keep a secret.'

George grinned at her.

'Well, will you?' she said.

'Maybe . . . when I can. I'm working most days.'

She got ready to open the door, then delayed.

'Can you do tricks?' she said.

'What kind of tricks?'

'*Tricks*. Dads are meant to do tricks.'

'Well, I'm not sure . . . D'you mean this kind of thing?'

He took a 10p coin from his pocket and made it pirouette along his fingers.

'Brilliant.' She was smiling, but it was something anybody could do.

'Go on, Jeanie.'

'See you, then.'

'Next time . . . when I can.'

He stared after her as she walked towards the house, feeling sad, feeling jubilant.

Chapter 15

Another day.

He had missed Jeanie, and was too early to meet Simone, so George was wasting time in his car, waiting for the auto-pager to summon him. He had been to High Holborn to see if a friend of his was around, and afterwards headed north to King's Cross.

He went to the bridge and drove along it, thinking that in the daylight it seemed bare and dreary, a nothing street, somewhere to get through as quickly as possible. Commuters were heading towards the station, heads down against the persistent drizzle, clutching newspapers and attaché cases and shoulder bags.

Halfway across, George jammed on his brakes. May was there, leaning languidly against the iron parapet, not even bothering to solicit the men who were hurrying past.

A few of them noticed her, though, because she looked so out of place. She was wearing the same clothes George had seen her in that night: the miniskirt, the see-through blouse, the black bra: the outfit that was meant to provoke sexual interest, but which made her look young and pathetic.

George's sudden braking got her interest, though, and she levered herself away from the parapet and walked in a dazed way across to him.

'Hello, darling,' she said. 'Looking for a good time?'

George leant over to her, and wound down the window.

'You're out early,' he said.

'I do the rush hour sometimes.' She had barely looked at him as she spoke. She had been intent on twisting her body in what she probably imagined was a provocative way, but had had to rest a hand on the bonnet of the car to keep her balance. Now she looked directly at him, and at once everything changed. 'It's *you*! You *told* him, didn't you?'

At the same instant George had seen that her face bore new bruises, inexpertly concealed with face powder and cream.

'Told him what?' he said automatically, but knew what she meant.

'Yeah, you told him, and he –'

She turned away in contempt, and walked off down the street, wobbling slightly on heels that were too high for her.

George reversed up past her, and stopped again.

When she drew level with the car he said: 'Come on, I didn't tell him!'

'*Fuck off!*' She carried on walking.

George leapt out of the car, ran after her and caught her.

'What do you want?' she said.

'Tell me what he did to you!'

'You know . . . he just took my gear, and then he –'

She started crying, and George put his forearms gently on her shoulders, not wanting to hug her properly for fear she would turn on him and fight him off.

'You told him, didn't you?' May said again.

'I saw him . . . he was right outside, like you said. I told him what a great time I'd had, that you'd made me happy.'

'He *knew* . . . you must have said something else.'

George looked anxiously at his car, sitting in the road with its engine running.

'Come on,' he said. 'We can't talk here. Let's get a cup of tea.'

'I don't drink tea.'

'Coffee then!'

'Would you buy me an ice cream?' Her clouded eyes looked anxiously at him, like those of a small pet animal that is learning how to manipulate humans, and George couldn't decide whether what she needed was sympathy and comfort, or a belt round the ear.

'All right, I'll get you an ice cream. Hop in the car.'

There was a cafe just around the corner in the next street. May followed him in, and they sat at a table next to the window. Looking out they could see the mouth of the road that crossed the bridge, grey and dismal in the rain.

'So what do you want then?' George said. 'Vanilla? Chocolate?'

'Knickerbocker Glory.'

'All right. Stay there.' He went to the counter, ordered the ice cream and a cup of tea for himself.

'What do you want?' May said.

'Just to talk.'

'You mean talk dirty?'

'I'm looking for someone I've got to find.'

102

'Who?'

'A friend of a friend. A girl like you. She's called Cathy.'

'My name's May.'

'Yeah . . . but you said you was a Cathy.'

'I say whatever you want.' She looked away, across at the road on the bridge. It was beginning to get dark. 'You sure you didn't tell him, Mister?'

'Cross my heart,' George said, miming the action.

'All right. I believe you.' She looked past him, over his shoulder, towards the counter. 'There's my ice cream.'

George got up from the table, and went to the counter. He had to fiddle around with the money; he didn't have enough change to pay the woman, and she made a fuss over changing his fiver. When he turned around, ice cream in one hand and tea in the other, May had gone.

He swore aloud, dumped the stuff on the table, and rushed out into the street. There was no sign of her. He looked along both roads, then crossed over through the rushing traffic and went towards the bridge. He had just reached the intersection when a car slowed for the corner, and turned into the traffic.

May was sitting in the back, staring vacantly out of the window. George moved quickly towards her, raising his hand.

The driver peered at him, and George felt a crackle of the man's malevolence. He recognised him at once: it was the large black man at the club, the one who called himself Smith.

Then it was Simone, and another night of driving and waiting, driving and waiting. The next afternoon, after a delivery, George went to the club behind Dean Street. The sign outside was not switched on, and no one stood at the door. He went inside, ready for trouble.

The only person he saw was Tim, who had taken him up the stairs to May. The man was sweeping the floor of the clubroom, a half-smoked cigarette stuck behind his ear.

'I've come about the girl,' George said.

The man looked up. 'What girl?'

'The girl, the fucking girl . . . the one called May. The little kid you had in the room up there.'

'She's gone.'

George was now at a pitch of anger. 'Where the fuck did she go?' he shouted.

'Don't ask me. They come and go all the time, mate.'

George grabbed him by the front of his shirt. 'But they have to go somewhere, don't they?'

The auto-pager in his pocket let out a bleep. He held the man for a few more seconds, then pushed him away.

The pager sounded again.

'Is that you making that noise, mate?' said Tim.

George strode over to him, fist raised.

'Just you fucking watch it. That's all.'

He pulled out the pager, flicked the button on the back, and put the thing back in his pocket.

He went to find a telephone.

Chapter 16

It was his third delivery that day, thankfully a small one. George left the car on a double yellow line, pulled the box out of the back of the car, slammed the lid, then went through into the shop. It was one he had never visited before: smaller than most, but brightly lit and with the empty boxes of the video tapes displayed rather attractively on clean shelves. By now, George was completely immune to the provocative photographs on the boxes: immense breasts, vulgar backsides and lasciviously extruded tongues . . . and outrageous titles promising all.

'Here,' George said. 'From the man.'

The youth standing by the till jerked his head towards a narrow door at the back of the shop.

'They go in there. Mick will sign for them.'

George went on through, having to turn sideways to get through the door with the carton in his arms.

Another man was sitting at a desk, with a pile of paperwork in front of him.

'Are you Mick?' George said.

'Yeah.'

'From the man.'

'How many?'

'No idea . . . a boxful.'

'Put them down there. I'll have to count them.'

George lowered the carton to the floor, then stepped back as Mick ripped open the tape that sealed the box, and started to take out the contents. George looked around the tiny room.

These places always had a room like this: the stuff out front was hard-core, or most of it was, and it was there for the average punter. The police routinely busted these places, and the tapes out front were the ones they took in, looked at, sometimes prosecuted over . . . and rarely returned. They usually weren't worth very much to start with: dupes of dupes of dupes, the titles and pictures on the boxes being arbitrary and interchangeable. Many of them were anyway faked up with photographs taken from magazines, and the punters never complained. So long as *something* was going on, and it was approximately what they were expecting, they would keep coming back for more.

The material in the back rooms, though, was different. In the first place it was rarely seized by the police, because it was not on public display. The story was that the back room was where they kept the tapes that had been wrongly delivered, waiting to be picked up. Or that they were for the personal use of the proprietor.

In reality, though, the back room was for the specialist customers, the rich and openly perverted. You only got into the back room on recommendation from someone known in the trade, or if you flashed a big enough wad at the kid on the front desk.

George always liked these glimpses when he was doing a delivery: the magazine covers were entirely explicit about their contents, and the contents did not disappoint those who looked inside them. George usually took the opportunity to browse through one or two, and they never failed to raise his eyebrows. What usually amazed him was the sheer level of specialisation: the obsessive attention to one sexual quirk or another, depicted and writ very large indeed.

And there were video tapes too. Unlike the ones in the front shops these rarely had photographic covers, and when they did they were usually in black and white. The titles were all that was needed; sometimes these were even written by hand. George had never actually sat down and watched one, but he had now been on the fringes of the trade long enough to know that what the tapes contained were moving equivalents of the photographs in the magazines. Highly detailed, totally explicit . . . and almost certainly too specialised for his own rather ordinary needs.

While Mick was counting the tapes he had just brought in, George wandered along the shelves, picking up a magazine or two, glancing at the tapes. He was beginning to grow as blasé about all this as he was about the tapes in the main shop.

Then one caught his attention: it had a small colour photograph on the box, which was unusual in itself, but this one had additional interest.

The picture showed a woman dressed in extremely tight and revealing leather underwear, holding a whip and a long metal chain, advancing on a naked man . . . who could only be seen in dark silhouette, looming huge and slightly out of focus at the front of the photograph.

The woman in the leather underwear was Simone.

George took the tape down, and looked more closely at it.

107

Behind him, Mick said: 'That's OK. They're all there.'

George turned around, and held up the tape.

'Can I borrow this for a while?' he said.

Mick shrugged. 'Suits me.'

'How much?'

'Take it. You're in the family, aren't you?'

'I think I must be,' George said, grinning. 'See you next time.'

As he went out the telephone on Mick's desk began to ring. George heard him say: 'Yes . . . yes.' Then: 'Here! Is your name George?' He nodded. 'It's for you.'

He took the receiver. 'Yeah, George here. All right. Where?'

He put it down again.

'They follow you everywhere, don't they?' said Mick.

He didn't have time to get back to the car, so he stopped at a newsagents and bought a large brown envelope. He slipped the video tape inside, then wrapped the paper tight around it and squeezed it into a pocket of his coat.

The address he had been given turned out to be one of the more plushy striptease joints in Soho. It bespoke pretension and middlebrow affectations to artistry: the pictures outside of the girls were tastefully airbrushed, or posed so that the parts of the body they were paid to reveal were not actually revealed, and the photographs were displayed in glass cabinets. The foyer of the joint had a fountain and pool full of fish, a box office that looked like something you would see in an Odeon, and there were thick carpets and heavy draperies everywhere. The lighting was . . . tasteful. If you had been encased in ice for two thousand years you might conceivably think you were entering a respectable little theatre or cinema.

George, who had not been so encased, strode through the foyer without a sideways glance, and pushed open the first door he saw that was marked PRIVATE.

Terry was there, waiting for him.

'They follow you everywhere, don't they?' he said.

'You're like a bad penny, you are,' George said. 'Where's your disinfectant today?'

'Don't need it in a place like this.'

'You work here too?'

'I get around,' Terry said.

'Yeah. Terry, look, about that girl.'

'What girl?'

'The kid . . . called May. The one you sent me up to, that you said was called Cathy.'

'What about her?'

'She's gone,' said George.

'No . . . I don't believe it.'

'Leave it out, Terry. Where is she?'

'You know what kids are like. One minute they're here, the next minute they're gone.' He gestured with his thumb, behind him. 'You'd better get upstairs. He's waiting for you.'

George stepped past him, then paused.

'Terry?' he said.

'Yeah.'

'There's something I'd like you to know.'

'What's that?'

'He phoned *me*.'

Mortwell was sitting backstage. Someone had put a little round table out for him, with a white cloth and an ice bucket. He was sitting in a monstrosity of a chair: it was made of shiny black leather, or PVC, and had been fashioned like a huge hand. As George walked up to him, he couldn't see the thumb, and he wondered where it went to.

The strippers – in this place they were probably described as 'artistes' – were on stage, rehearsing a dance routine. Mortwell was watching them with detached interest, pulling on a long cigar. Because of the time of day the girls looked like working dancers, not like paid sex objects, and they were clad in leotards, leg warmers and dancing shoes. Their feet made a muffled clumping sound on the bare boards of the stage, as they practised their steps.

Mortwell saw George approaching.

'Hiya, George.'

'Hello, Dinny.'

'Sit down somewhere . . . how's the missus?'

'Don't see her much any more.'

'The kid then?'

'She's fine.'

Mortwell leaned forward and pulled a large green champagne bottle out of the ice bucket. He gestured with it to George.

'It's my birthday today . . . you know that? My fucking birthday.'

'Happy birthday,' said George, in a flat voice.

'Aren't you going to ask me how old I am?'

'How old are you, Dinny?'

'Fifty-two, George. Fifty-two. And you?'

'It's not my birthday.'

'Have a drink anyway.'

There was a spare glass on the table, which Mortwell filled with a generous quantity of champagne, then passed to George. He topped up his own glass.

'Cigar?'

'No thanks.'

'You know what I think, George?'

'What do you think?'

'I think that you think I left you in the shit.'

'Well you did, didn't you? Kind of.'

'Life keeps on happening, George. We can't control it. We can only swim in it.'

'Yeah . . . but what happens if you can't swim?'

'Water on the brain.' Mortwell tapped the side of his head in a significant way.

'That can't be good, Dinny.'

'You know what happens then?'

'What happens?'

'You get yourself confused, George. And always over the little things. You know the little things . . .?'

'What little things?' Mortwell had always done this to him, talked in riddles.

'I mean,' Mortwell said. 'Do you or do you not get confused?'

'Oh yeah. I get confused.'

'You still get confused. Great. But at least now you know, don't you, George?'

'Now I know.'

'And that's something . . . because you know what I'm good at?'

'What?' said George, tiring of this.

'I'm good at the little things. Little things that mean everything. The things you forget. And I've got a family now, all perfectly legal. All through the little things. And you're part of that family, George. One of my favourite parts.'

'I'm glad to hear that, Dinny.'

'I thought you would be. Have some more champagne.'

'No thanks. I still haven't finished this.'

'Have you seen round the place yet?'

'I only just got here.'

'Let me show you. You'll like this . . . it's got real class.'

George followed Mortwell through the wings, and out on to the stage. The girls continued their rehearsal around them, whirling and clumping in rhythm. Mortwell pointed out all the paraphernalia he was proud of: trapdoors set in the stage, smoke effects, special lighting, a laser system. George nodded and nodded, trying to look interested . . . all this just for girls to flash their pubic hair at silent men they could hardly see, out there in the dark anonymity of the tiny auditorium.

At length they headed back to Mortwell's table.

George said: 'So what's it all about, Dinny?'

'You're *happy*, that's what it's all about. You served your time, you came out. I wasn't here, now I am here. I want you to know that I know that.'

'I know that,' said George.

'So you're busy, you got a job. Any complaints?'

'No.'

'That girl you're with, the one you drive around. She sees the Arab.'

'Every night.'

'Do you ever ask her what she does?'

'What do you mean?' said George. 'What *he* does?'

'I mean what she does. What does he pay her to do?'

'I've no idea.'

'Then ask her.'

'Why me?' said George.

'Because you drive her. You should be looking at these things, little things. It's a different business, George, but the rules are the same. How could I ask her that?'

'Same way as me, I expect.'

'No . . . this is a little thing I want you to do. Get her to tell you – truthfully, mind. Get her to tell you, and then you tell me. And I'll be happy. Like you, George. Right?'

He rose from his outlandish chair, and placed his cigar in the ashtray. George, picking up the signal, stood up too. Mortwell put a comradely arm around his shoulder, and led him towards the exit.

'You didn't like me in the old days, did you?' Mortwell said. George looked at him sharply. 'Don't worry . . . everybody hates me once in a while. But all that's changed, I know. It's now important to me that you should be happy, George.'

'That's all right, Dinny. Everyone I meet makes me happy these days.'

Chapter 17

They were halfway through the long evening. Two appointments behind her, three or four ahead of her, Simone had issued the now familiar direction: 'St John's Wood.'

Seeing no point in beating about the bush, George said: 'What do you get up to with him?'

'With who?'

'King Faisal.'

'I told you a hundred times. None of your business.'

'Depends on your point of view. My business is driving you around. And anyway, you said I was curious.'

'Curious . . . or just plain nosey?'

'Interested.'

'All right,' she said. 'What do you *think* I do with him?'

'You know . . . a bit of the other.'

'OK. Then why ask?'

'I mean . . . what do you actually *do*?'

'You won't like it.'

'Try me.'

Simone stared ahead at the road.

'I drink tea with him,' she said.

George snorted, and banged his hands on the crossbar of the steering wheel.

'Don't make fun of me!' he said.

'What's this all about, George?'

'I was asked to find out. I thought the best way was to ask you straight out.'

'Who asked you?'

'Your boss.'

'I don't have a boss.'

'Yes you do. Same as mine . . . Mortwell.'

They had reached the familiar house, and George went up the drive, the gravel crunching under the tyres. He pulled to a halt on the apron.

Simone said: 'Tell your Mr Mortwell that I drink tea.' She opened the door and got out. Holding the door open, she looked back at him. 'Twenty minutes.'

'All right, all right. Just hope the water's boiled.'

She walked across the gravel, to be met at the door by the white-coated servant. The door closed on her.

George settled down to wait, feeling disagreeable.

About five minutes later he heard the measured tread of the servant on the gravel, and he sat up expectantly. The servant halted by the car door, the silver tray balanced on the fingers of his hand.

'Madame wished me to bring you this, sir,' he said.

He lowered the tray, and George saw that it held two Polaroid snapshots. He picked them from the tray, and switched on the light. The servant departed.

Simone and the Arab were seated together on a huge couch draped with ornate tapestries. The room, or that part of it visible in the picture, was sumptuously furnished and decorated. She was wearing her glittery dress; he was in an immaculate business suit. They were smiling at each other in one photograph; in the other they were smiling at the camera. In both pictures there was a golden teapot with a long spout standing on the low table in front of them, and they were holding bone-white china teacups.

George propped up the photographs on the dashboard, but beyond that neither of them referred to the incident until the end of the evening.

When he had parked the car outside her block of flats, George said: 'So what does Mortwell want?'

'He wants to win friends and influence people.'

'How does he go about that?'

'Through girls like me. Goodnight, George.'

Simone had opened her door.

'Can I come up with you. I've something to show you.'

'What? Or is that a line?'

'I don't need a line,' George said. 'I want to show you something inside.'

'All right . . . but you can't stay long. I'm tired.'

Inside the flat Simone lit the gas fire, then went through to her bedroom to change. When she had her robe on, she said: 'Would you like something to drink?'

'A cup of tea?' He grinned at her.

'I'll make you tea if you want it.'

She went into the kitchen, ran water, and made noises with crockery. While she was out there George removed the video tape from his pocket, then crumpled up and threw away the envelope he had wrapped it in. He switched on Simone's video recorder and TV set, and slotted the tape in.

'What are you going to show me?' Simone called from the kitchen.

'I'm getting it ready. You see, I do deliveries when I'm not out pimping for you.'

'You're not pimping for me.'

'What is it then?'

She came in with a tray with tea and cups and saucers. She set them down on a low table.

'What kind of deliveries do you do?'

'This kind,' George said, and using the remote control switched on the tape player. He had not checked to see if the tape had been fully rewound, and the picture came on in the middle of the action.

What was going on was a rough approximation of the picture on the box. Simone – presumably a year or two younger, but looking much the same as she did now – was wearing tight-fitting leather underwear, although not quite as much as in the picture. She was in a passionate clinch with a black man, although the camera was so close you could see nothing more of him than the flat wall of his stomach and his bulging jeans. Simone was caressing the bulge, then with nimble fingers flicked the top button apart and unzipped him. As his swollen penis came into view she took it greedily into her mouth.

The camera cut away briefly to the man's face. It was the man George had met at the club. Smith, Mr Smith.

He and Simone stared at the screen, each with their own horrified reactions.

Simone was the first to speak. *'Turn it off!'* she shouted.

George was slow to move. Simone reached across him, seized the remote control and with a quick, furious action switched it off.

'Fuck you, you bastard! Oh you *bastard*!'

George was stunned.

'Where the hell did you get this tape?' she said.

'I told you . . . I do deliveries. This stuff.'

'I never thought –'

George said: 'Who *is* that man?'

'What does it matter who he is? It's just me and a piece of meat.'

'He said he was called Smith. I've seen him around.'

'His real name's Anderson.'

'You mean that's *Anderson*? Your ponce?' He stood up, moved away from her. 'Jesus! Why am I in all this?'

'I told you,' Simone said, 'because I asked you.'

'That's not why.'

'And because you like me, and you fancy me. Don't bother to deny it. I might be a tart but I'm not a stupid tart! You could have me, George, but that's nothing. Any prick in London can have me.'

'Shut up!' George said, angrily.

'My job is to get screwed. I get screwed by everyone I meet. Usually I'm screwed by old men with trusses, and they're so fat I have to lift myself on to them.'

Taken by his anger, George turned on her and hit her full across the face. She gasped, and staggered back. Then she recovered, and immediately returned the blow. She caught him with her fist clenched, and the impact on the side of his face hurt him more than he could have believed possible. He ducked away from her, holding his head.

'Don't hit me, George, don't *ever* hit me again! Nobody hits me. They can have me any way they like. They can degrade me, abuse me, call me a nigger whore, make me do to them anything the perverted bastards can dream up . . . but they can't hit me. That fucker Anderson was the one who decided me. He hit me. Again and again, every day and every hour of every day he hit me, whenever he had a spare minute.'

George lowered his hand, humbled by the sudden pain, and by her fury.

'I'm sorry, Simone,' he said.

'You don't understand, do you?'

'No . . . I don't understand.' She too had recovered, shaken down by the outburst into trembling calmness. 'What don't I understand?'

'About Anderson. There are people who like that kind of thing, who want to cause pain. Real pain, real suffering. They pay him to get it for them. If he has Cathy, anyone can have her . . . for anything they want.'

'I thought that was the idea.'

'I mean anyone. Any sadistic bastard who likes little girls. They'll kill her in the end.'

They were both worn out, and stared wordlessly at each other. George at last began to realise the urgency of the search she had sent him on, and the difficulty of it for him . . . and the danger for her, without him.

At last he said: 'Here . . . drink your tea.'

He passed her the cup, but as soon as she had hold

119

of it she flung it violently at the television set. It hit the screen full on; the cup broke, but the screen did not. Brown tea trickled down on to the carpet.

She looked at George, and let out a laugh, suppressing it inadequately so that it sounded like a snort.

'That's the girl,' George said. He picked up the other cup and gave it to her. 'Try this one instead.'

Chapter 18

It had been a week since George had managed to get away in time, but now he was back, waiting outside the school in Wandsworth. Just to be sure she wouldn't miss him he stood outside the car, resting his backside against the wing, arms folded.

It was a blue, bright day, cooler than it had been recently. George was perplexed with his life, with Simone, with Mortwell, with the search he had agreed to undertake. None of it was getting him anywhere, although he was at least being paid. It was good to have money again.

Jeanie provided the only real constant in his life: she was all he was sure of. Although she was in some ways the least accessible part of his life, at the same time she provided him with his only sense of a future. He loved her fiercely, wanted to love her more.

And Simone. . . .

He was starting to love her too, and even said the word to himself before kicking it away in his mind. She tantalised and tormented him, almost out of habit, so used was she to the way men abused her. He was caught in the crossfire night after night, as her defences blazed away, and even as he ducked and weaved – and, he knew, drew the fire to himself – her sheer perversity of spirit made her irresistible to him.

Yet he had his own perversity too: he was more jealous of her past than of her present. As she went her tireless round, hotel to hotel, expensive house to rented villa, drinking tea or whatever it was she *really* did, George sat phlegmatically in his car or hotel lounge, nursing no resentment.

But he brooded about her past, about Anderson and Cathy, Mortwell and Terry and the other shades, shifting behind her. Somehow, it was acceptable that she should lead her dangerous life while he was there to oversee it, but the thought that she had been doing this in the past troubled him in ways he could not fully comprehend.

For all this, Jeanie steadied him. When she appeared amongst the crowd of hastily departing schoolkids, he smiled at her happily. She came over to him, abandoning her friends.

'Where have you been, Dad?' she said.

'Busy . . . sorry. I said I couldn't make it every day.' They both climbed in.

'I know. But –'

'Look at them,' George said, pointing to her friends. 'They still jealous?'

'I hope so.'

He got the car moving, and tried to find an even longer way back to her house.

'Did you tell her?' he said.

'Mum? No . . . but she guessed.'

'How?'

'She always knows.'

'Mothers always do. Especially yours.'

Jeanie was staring into her lap, playing with the carrying strap of her bag.

'See, I asked her about you.'

'You shouldn't have.'

'She said that too.'

George glanced away from the road; looked at her. She was staring at him very earnestly. The sight of her sent another pang through him.

'What's wrong with you, then?' she said.

'What do you think?'

'I don't know you.' She grinned at him. 'You seem OK to me.'

'Listen, I'm tired and I'm getting old, and I didn't treat your Mum right.'

'How didn't you treat her right?'

'I forgot she was there, y'know. Funny, that.'

'And I forgot you were there, until the other day.'

He put it off as long as he could, but then he set a world record: Mortwell called him. A second time.

They met in the same place, but the artistes were absent. Mortwell was in an edgy, dangerous mood. George recognised it from the old days, and it made him feel more at ease. When Dinny was pretending to be his friend, head of his family, he knew there was a catch. He had wanted something from George, and George had kept him waiting.

Mortwell was sitting alone in the cramped auditorium when George arrived. The stage was spotlit, a splash of white light, drawing attention to itself, distracting like the screen of a television set with the sound turned off.

'Tell me, George,' he said.

'What about?'

'Don't fuck about with me. About the whore you drive around.'

'Nothing, Dinny.'

'What do you mean, nothing?'

'I mean nothing. The opposite of something.'

'She goes to his house every night and does *nothing*? Do you think I'm as stupid as you?'

'She drinks tea with him.'

Mortwell gave a short, sardonic laugh. 'She's lying.'

'Why would she do that?' George said.

'Don't know. Find out for me.'

'How am I gonna do that?'

'That's up to you. Climb a drainpipe, hide in a wardrobe. Take a picture . . . but find out.'

'I've got a picture, Dinny.'

He took the two Polaroid photos from his pocket, and handed them to Mortwell.

A few yards away from them a stripper walked silently on to the stage, wearing a lavish costume of boa feathers and sequins. She stood still in the motionless spotlight, but then began to pace the stage. In a moment, she was moving rhythmically, as if to imagined music. As the pacing transformed itself to dance, her body seemed more supple, more fluid. She began to strip off the costume, with expert, economical movements of her limbs.

Mortwell did not even glance in her direction. He stared at the photographs for a few seconds, then his eyes flashed back at George.

'You trying to be funny with me, George?'

'I told you, Dinny. She goes in the house and drinks tea.'

Mortwell rose from his seat, very suddenly, making George think he was about to be struck. He stood his ground, facing Mortwell. But Mortwell smiled at him, a level, unpleasant smile.

'You are funny, Georgie. You know that?'

'Yeah. I suppose I am.'

On the stage, the girl had stripped down to sequinned bra and G-string, and was now using one of the boa feathers to caress herself suggestively.

'Get something better,' Mortwell said.

'How do you mean . . . better?'

'I mean dirty, George. I mean nasty. Kinky, slimy, perverted. Anything you like . . . but not tea.'

Terry had appeared quietly, and was standing a few feet away.

'He's waiting, Dinny,' he said.

Mortwell turned, and so did George. A man was standing in the shadows close to the stage, staring up at the stripper. She had removed her bra, and as they watched she slipped out of the G-string. The imagined music in her mind must have ceased, because she stopped dancing and walked to the front of the stage.

Standing in the full glare of the spotlight, pale and slim and pretty, with a soft scut of ginger hair and large pink nipples, she called out: 'How was that, Mr Mortwell?'

Mortwell was looking at the man in the shadows. He said, without so much as moving his eyes: 'Perfect, darlin', perfect.' He moved away from George, weaving down through the seats. Then he paused, looked back.

'You got that then, George?' he said.

'All right.'

'Do it.'

Then George was forgotten as Mortwell went to the other man. He stepped forward to meet Mortwell, and part of the spotlight beam fell on him. It was Anderson.

Mortwell greeted him like a long-lost brother, hugging and slapping him on the back.

Anderson stared past him, into the auditorium, directly at George.

That night, very late indeed, George was alert and frightened, totally incapable of sleep. Thomas, unexpectedly, had been out when he came in, so George had taken the opportunity to prowl restlessly around the studio, working off the animal tension that had been growing in him all day.

Then Thomas had come in, and George pretended to have only just arrived home himself. Thomas soon declared his intention of going to bed to read, and George stayed at his own end of the caravan, his mind still churning.

In the end he dug out the video tape, and slotted it into Thomas's machine. He ran the tape from the beginning, and kept the volume turned off, watching the flickering images in silence. The tape was not a long one: maybe twenty-five minutes in all. When it was finished he wound it back, and when he came to the scene with Anderson he froze the frame on the man's face.

Thomas said: 'Until you did that I thought you were watching Channel 4.'

George turned in surprise.

'How long have you been sitting there?' he said.

'Long enough.'

Thomas had left his bunk, and was sitting in the one easy chair, which they kept in the central area of the caravan.

'You saw all that, then?' George said.

'I did.' Thomas came over to him, and sat on the bunk beside him. 'What's wrong, George? You can't even finish reading a novel these days, but you can look at crap like that. You used to be my hero. What's happening?'

'Your hero?' George said, pleased.

'Well, you know . . .'

'Can you get your hero a gun, then?'

'What did you just say?'

'A gun. A shooter.'

'Jesus, what do you want that for?'

George gave him a look of mock contempt.

Then he said: 'Remember the horse that was murdered?'

'Yes.'

'Well, I did it. And the lawyer's wife was very upset.'

'You're not joking about this, are you?' Thomas said. 'About the gun.'

'When did I ever make jokes?'

'You used to have one about a randy gorilla.'

'No one ever laughed at that,' George said, remembering then.

'It's the way you tell them.'

Simone came out of the lift, walked towards him, and they went through the charade of greeting each other like man and wife.

Then she said quietly: 'Come on . . . I'm late again.'

'I need to know something,' George said.

'Can't it wait?'

'What does he use, your Anderson?'

'A blade.'

'Does he ever use a shooter?'

'Not as far as I know.'

George presented her with his arm, and they walked across the hotel lobby towards the door.

Simone said: 'Why do you ask?'

'Doesn't matter. Where to now?'

'The Lambert.' They were out in the street. After a glance backwards she said: 'And fucking hurry.'

The next day he did his rounds as quickly as he could, and by three-thirty had completed them all. Throughout the day he had rationalised his haste by telling himself he wanted to get down to Wandsworth, but when the time came he walked off into Soho.

He found Mortwell's strip club, and hung around outside. The club was in a building that abutted on to a street market, so George was able to loiter without drawing too much attention to himself. After half an hour, his patience was rewarded: Anderson came out of the club and walked off purposefully down the street.

George followed.

Anderson did not go very far: his car was parked illegally on a meter with a yellow cover pulled over the display. As he fiddled with the door and opened it, George hared off to where he had left his own car.

The congested one-way streets of Soho played to

George's advantage, and within a couple of minutes he had relocated Anderson's car. By ducking through an alley where he often made deliveries, George was able to keep the man in sight, separated by two or three cars.

In this way they drove together towards Kilburn High Road. When Anderson parked, George pulled over to the side to see where he was going. The man went without a sideways look towards a narrow, white-painted door, and entered. George drove off to find somewhere to park the Jaguar.

The place was a men-only Turkish bath and sauna. After only a moment's hesitation, George went inside. There was a pay desk, staffed by a short and muscular man, dressed in a white T-shirt and the lower half of a track suit.

'How much?' George said.

'You a member?'

'No.'

'Three pounds twenty, then.'

George paid up, and was given a flannelette dressing gown and a huge white towel.

A few minutes later, clad in the dressing gown and with the towel draped around his neck, George went to explore the bathhouse. It was larger than he had expected, as it extended into a wide basement. There were numerous saunas and massage tables, an exercise gym, an impressive row of Turkish baths, and three pools: a small and a large cold plunge, and a hot pool. Much of the place was filled with drifting steam.

It was the sort of place where people kept themselves to themselves, and although many men were using the facilities, very few of them even glanced at him. Many sat naked in the heat, reading newspapers or resting with eyes closed, while inside the saunas there was not much to do but sit and sweat and contemplate inwardly.

He soon found Anderson: he was with Mortwell, and both men lay naked in the shallows of the hot pool, gripping the side rail and letting their bodies float languidly in the water.

George stepped past them unseen, and hovered within earshot.

Mortwell told a joke, then another, then another. Anderson did not laugh once. George thought they were fairly good jokes, worth more than a silent response.

Later, when the two men started swimming around, George wandered away before they noticed him.

He saw Anderson later in the changing rooms, but the man was showering and did not see him. George dressed quickly, and went outside to wait.

Within ten minutes, George was involved in another shadowing drive across London: he should have thought of this beforehand, because it was easy to lose someone in London. On the other hand, he had always been paid for his driving. A top driver was what he was, or what he had been before he took the rap for Mortwell.

Surprising him, Anderson took a sudden turn into a small sidestreet. It happened so quickly that George's instant reaction was that he had been spotted . . . but as he passed the end of the street he saw that Anderson had simply noticed a vacant place to park. George, lacking the same luck, parked illegally and hurried back. He was in time to see Anderson's unmistakable and athletic figure walk around a corner into another back road.

It was a street with close-packed buildings, and at first George thought he had lost his quarry. He walked along the road quite openly, making no attempt to conceal himself, and looked for any place the man could have gone. There were several private houses, and of course he could have entered any of these. George was loth to start ringing doorbells and asking for him . . .

But then he noticed the church.

It was a short distance from the intersection where he had last seen Anderson, and the man could conceivably have got inside. Without pausing to wonder why he should enter a church on a weekday afternoon, or what would happen if Anderson really were inside, George walked quickly across and went through the open door.

He slowed his pace once he was inside, unexpectedly awed by the solemn architecture and the aura of reverence.

The church was empty, but for one person. It was a young woman sitting in a pew towards the front of the church. Her posture was erect, and her head was raised. She was smoking a cigarette.

George went to sit in the row behind her.

He said: 'I don't think you should smoke in a place like this.'

She made no answer, but stared straight ahead. She raised her cigarette for another puff, and as she did so George saw the back of her right hand. There was a tattoo there: two concentric hearts, pricked in blue.

'Cathy . . .?'

She turned then to look at him, and her eyes had a vague, glassy look.

'Is your name Cathy?' he said again.

She said nothing, thin smoke being expelled slowly from her nostrils. Her face was frightened.

'Put your cigarette out,' he said, in as kind a voice as he could manage. Some atavistic respect for the church had risen in him, and the sight and smell of the cigarette jarred on his nerves.

Wordlessly, she rose from her seat and went to a small cluster of votive candles. She carelessly stubbed out the cigarette in the soft wax of the top of one of them.

Cathy moved away from him, edging through the narrow aisle at the side of the pews. She looked back at him, still scared of him and his unexplained knowledge of her.

All he could think was how young she looked, how fragile, how translucently beautiful . . . and how empty of life she seemed.

Not wishing to be seen to pursue her directly, George walked the other way, down the central nave towards the chancel, intending to intercept her before she reached the door. But there was a raised pulpit he had to take a detour around, and on the far side of this he found his way blocked.

By the time he returned to the central part of the church she had vanished.

Abandoning his rediscovered respect for the cloth, George ran down the nave and reached the open door.

Anderson was there with Cathy.

He was leading her down the street, a hand resting lightly on the back of her neck.

She walked with him to his car, climbed into it, and sat in silence as Anderson started the engine.

They drove away, passing George on the corner of the street. Cathy stared ahead, into some remote, private distance.

Chapter 19

He knew where Simone was going to be: that was now their arrangement for the early part of the evenings. She made her way to the appointment by herself, and he guaranteed to be there by a certain time, ready to drive her away.

It was the hotel in Cumberland Gate. They had both been growing increasingly paranoid about the hotel detective, whose suspicions and aggravating behaviour were now a regular feature of their visits. Once, Simone had said to George in the car that if it continued she would either have to start operating somewhere else, or bring him formally into the system. Meanwhile, because she wanted to do neither, Simone was carrying on as long as she could, trying to avoid the detective as often as possible.

She had started telling George the number of the room she would be in; a last-ditch recourse, in which if absolutely pressed he could call up to the room and signal the alarm. He had never had to do so yet, and Simone had only very grudgingly agreed to this . . . saying she could not imagine what scale of emergency would justify it. But he was growing as nervous of the hotel as she was, and had insisted.

There was no sign of the detective as George hurried in. The waiter in the pigtail was on duty as usual, nodded to George as he went rushing past, and took his pen from his pocket. But George went straight to the lifts, hit the button, and stood impatiently while he waited for the lift car to reach him.

He reached into his back trousers pocket, and pulled out the slip of paper on which he had earlier scribbled the room number.

When the car arrived George moved quickly inside, pressed the button for the sixth floor, then had to stand while the mechanism went through its slow process of deciding to obey him. Mushy orchestral music tinkled at him from a hidden loudspeaker, and on the car wall were glossy blandishments for the hotel's restaurants: a grill, a bistro, a five-star international cuisinerie. Two American ladies with blue-rinsed hair joined him in the car, discussing their day trip to Stratford-on-Avon. They pressed the button for the fourth floor.

The sixth floor was almost deserted when George arrived: he had to look for the signs leading him to the corridor containing Room 631, and pushed through numerous fire doors to find it. A maid was there, wheeling a trolley of soiled sheets towards the house-keeper's room.

George strolled past her, trying to look as if he was going somewhere else. He waited behind another fire door until she had moved out of sight.

When the coast was clear, he went straight to the door of the room, and rapped on it with his knuckles.

A long silence followed. He tried again.

Then, from just behind the door, a male voice said: 'What do you want?'

'Service,' George said.

'We didn't order any.'

'Open the door!' He again banged his fist against the door.

Another pause, then there was a rattling noise. The door opened, secured by a chain. The face of an elderly man peered through the chink.

'What –?'

The moment he saw George, he ducked back out of sight and the door started closing.

George wasted no time. He threw his weight against the door, heard a cracking noise, and saw that the wood of the frame had started to crack around the chain bracket. Before the man inside could close the door, George barged against it once more: the wood splintered, and the door banged open. The man in the room was thrown backwards by this, and as George stumbled through he almost tripped over the man's prostrate body.

He was wearing a white singlet, and loose-fitting striped drawers. He had socks on. He was an old man, grey and wrinkled, his flesh loose and pink, withered with age. He tried to scramble away from George, then changed his mind and lunged at him, trying to catch his legs and bring him to the ground.

'Get out of the fucking way!' George shouted, but the old man clung on to his leg, pulling at the fabric of his trousers.

They were still in the short corridor leading from the door into the main part of the room, and so far George had seen no sign of Simone.

The man started howling, so George turned his attention full on him. With a practised movement he booted the man in his stomach, hard enough to hurt, but not enough to injure.

At last he was released, and he scrambled on into the main room. He saw Simone at once.

She was on the bed, naked and bound.

The man had gagged her and blindfolded her, then pulled her head back so that her neck was bent at an excruciating angle. Her arms were stretched back past her head, and tied tightly to the headboard of the bed. Her ankles too had been bound, and her legs were stretched wide apart, tied with scarves to the feet of the bed. She was struggling feebly against these restraints.

A streak of silvery semen dribbled across her taut stomach, filtering wetly into her pubic hair. Another damp stain lay stickily on the gag across her mouth.

George said, hoarsely and stupidly: 'Simone . . .?'

He crossed to her, and released the blindfold. Struggling still, she stared up at him, her eyes wide with surprise.

'Jesus!' George said. Simone arched her back, fighting against the bonds.

Behind him, the man had recovered. He came into the room, groped for a pair of spectacles lying on the bedside table, and put them on.

He said: 'You bloody thug! How dare you –'

George looked at him contemptuously. Now the man was wearing glasses, George briefly glimpsed him in his other life. He visualised a business suit, a company car, panelled boardrooms, merchant banks, takeover bids, an office with Chairman inscribed on the door.

George punched the man, again aiming for the stomach.

'And fuck you too,' he shouted.

The man gasped and doubled up, reeling away across the room.

George bent over Simone, and ripped away the gag.

The moment she was free, she yelled: 'George! Get the hell out of here!'

'It's OK, I'll get you untied.'

'*Fuck off George!* I'm working!'

Suddenly he realised what had been going on.

He said: 'God, I'm sorry. I didn't mean –'

'Get him his glasses.'

George looked at the man, who was squatting painfully by the wall, trying to catch his breath. His spectacles had fallen off when George punched him, and he was groping on the carpet for them. George moved towards him, felt something snap beneath his foot, and realised he had stepped on them.

'Oh, fuck!' George said. He bent down, picked up the glasses and held them up to the light: a starfish of cracks had appeared on one lens. Humbly, he passed them to the man.

Once again, the reunion of the man with his glasses seem to inspire him. Peering uncertainly through the crazed lens, he stood up. Ignoring George, he moved to the side of the bed and stood over Simone.

'You told me you were respectable,' he said angrily.

'I am fucking respectable,' she said.

'You black bitch, you bloody whore . . .'

'Mind your damned language!' George said.

'Keep out of this, pimp.'

George slugged the man again, and as he crumpled weakly George kicked at him. The man fell to the floor, and rolled away.

'Who is this prat?' George said to Simone. 'I hate the sight of him.'

'Stop it, George. Fucking *stop it*! Help him up.'

From the floor the man screamed: 'I'll get the police up here, you bloody animals.'

'That does it!' George cried. 'I warned you, didn't I?'

He stooped over the man, got his arm wrested behind his back, then pulled and kicked him down the short passage. The man was on his knees by the time George got him to the door. He was propelled into the outside corridor with the flat of George's shoe.

George slammed the door, and somewhat surprisingly the lock clicked.

He returned to the bed, and started releasing Simone's limbs.

She said: 'Jesus Christ, George. You really are a stupid bastard!'

'I found her,' George said.

'Don't you ever, *ever*, do that again!'

'I said I found her. I found Cathy.'

She was suddenly alert, and as her legs came free she sat up on the bed.

'Where is she?'

'I don't know . . . but I can find her again.'

From beyond the door they heard the man shouting to be let in.

George looked once more at Simone's beautiful naked body, then found the small bundle of her clothes.

'Here,' he said. 'You'd better get dressed.'

'I've got to clean up first.'

'No time for that. The management will be here at any moment.'

'Yes, but –'

'Just make yourself look respectable. That's what it's all about, isn't it? Respectable?'

Simone moved with admirable swiftness, pulling on her scanty underwear and minuscule dress in a matter of seconds. She paused to run her fingers through her hair, then got her coat on.

A small wad of ten-pound notes sat on the dressing table, bound up in an elastic band. Simone picked them up, and stuffed them in her pocket.

Outside, the man had started kicking at the door.

'Here, that's stealing,' George said.

'No . . . it's a fee. He got what he wanted . . . or most of it.'

'Come on, let's go!'

George pulled the door open, and the man was there, his broken eyeglasses glinting at them. As soon as he saw George he backed away, colliding with the maid, who had evidently hurried down the corridor to find out what was going on.

She saw George and Simone.

'Is anything the matter, sir?' she said to George.

George looked at the pathetic old man with disgust.

'What's going on out here?' he said.

'I think I'd better call the manager,' the maid said, and scuttled away.

'It's a disgrace,' George said, and offered his arm to Simone. 'Come along, dear.'

With an evil grin at the man, he carefully closed the door, then he and Simone walked away.

In the lift, George said: 'That what you do every night?'

'Stop it, George! He's one of my regulars. Or he was.'

140

But she had not released his arm, as if she recognised his actions had finally closed off any possibility, however remote, of her ever returning to this place.

Crossing the lobby, she said: 'Where is Cathy?'

'In a hotel, tied to a four-poster bed.'

'Don't mess, George.'

'Same as you.'

'It's my fucking job.'

'Hers too, from what you said.'

They walked through the revolving door, and Simone took his arm again. But as they were about to go down the steps to the car park, the hotel detective stepped out of the shadows and grabbed Simone by the elbow.

'Just a minute, you!' he said loudly.

'Get off.' She tried to wrench herself free.

'One minute, miss.'

'Let me go. Don't touch me!'

'Get your hands off her!' George said.

'Shut your face.' He said to Simone: 'Look, I know what you're up to.'

'Don't keep touching me. Who the hell do you think you are?'

'I told you, get your hands off my wife!' George said.

'I want to look in her bag. What you got in there?'

Simone suddenly relented.

'All right,' she said. 'Let go of my arm, and I'll show you.'

'In the light, now. Where I can see you.'

'He's got no right to search you!' George said.

'It's all right, dear. I've nothing to hide.'

The three of them stepped back to the door, and the detective released her arm.

Simone said: 'Look, I know what you want. How much?'

'Half . . . and make it quick.'

'Are you crazy?' George said.

'I know what I'm doing, George.' To the detective: 'Half every time?'

'Just give me the money.'

Simone opened her bag, dipped a hand into it and came out an instant later holding a small black aerosol spray.

'It's all yours,' she said, and squirted a fine, high-pressure spray straight into his face.

The man lurched back, clutching his eyes. He bent over, roaring with pain and staggering helplessly against the wall of the hotel.

'Come on, George!'

They turned and ran to the car. Once away, driving quickly, George said: 'What the hell was that?'

'Mace.'

'Jesus, you don't need *anyone*, do you?'

'I do. I need you. Tell me about Cathy . . . where is she?'

'With your friend Anderson.'

'Where was she?'

'In a church. Why did he meet her there?'

'It's the one place no one goes,' Simone said.

George glanced at her; tears were trickling down her cheeks.

'Where to?' he said.

'Tonight . . . I just want to go home.'

Chapter 20

It was unusual to be driving to Islington so early. They
normally went back to Simone's flat after midnight
when the traffic was lighter, and subtly different in
kind. London changed when the small hours arrived:
unseen by most people, it was seedier, darker, more
furtive. Instead of the familiar black taxi-cabs there
were minicabs, instead of buses and lorries there were
unmarked vans, and instead of ordinary cars there
were black Daimlers and Rolls-Royces, with rich people in the back. All this had become George's driving
environment, and he identified it now with Simone. It
felt strange and difficult to have her beside him while
dealing with the frustrations of driving in normal
traffic: she had become a personal symbol of the alternative, late-night London.

She distracted him from everything. The anger that
had seized him in the hotel room had been transmuted
to a calm tenderness. He saw the client she had been
with as a pathetic victim of something or other – his
impulses, his greed – and George was already sorry
for what he had done to him. But at the same time his
natural sense of individuality rejected any temp-
tations towards showing either tenderness or con-
trition, and when he and Simone spoke they did so in
their usual barbed terms.

Something had changed, though. Had he barged into the room that way in their early days together, his life would not now be worth living: if she had not literally lacerated him with her nails or any other weapon that came to hand, she would have done so figuratively with the sharpest edge of her tongue, and he would genuinely now be out of a job. Certainly she would not have been sitting with him in his car, as they drove resignedly towards her flat. They were better together now, a team, a couple of partners, acting in accord.

But it was a clumsy, prickly accord: two misfits of different kinds, managing to make it work somehow. For George, it was all confused by the powerful infatuation he felt, something that now made him dizzy whenever he was with her, yet one which he resisted with a steely, contradictory determination.

They came at last to her street. Simone was slumping in the passenger seat beside him, all the nervous energy gone temporarily from her. George drove slowly, looking for somewhere to park.

He braked suddenly, jerking Simone back into attention.

'What's the matter?' she said.

'See that car there? Do you recognise it?'

She looked where he was pointing: a large, dark-coloured saloon was parked a short distance away from the entrance to the flats.

'What about it?'

'I think it's Anderson's car.'

'Shit . . . Are you sure?'

'I've been following one like it all afternoon.'

'It can't be. He doesn't know where I live. How do you know it's his?'

'I just told you.'

'Is it the same number plate?'

George eased up the clutch and moved his car slowly forward, until the number plate came into view. He frowned.

'Now I'm not sure,' he said. 'I think that's the same number . . . it looks like it.'

He accelerated away, and took a left turn.

'What shall we do?' he said.

'Drive around the block. Let me think.'

'Have you ever seen that car before?'

'I think so. It might belong to someone who lives in the street.'

George took another left, and drove slowly along until he came to Essex Road again. Here he paused, letting the engine idle.

'Well, does it or doesn't it?' he said.

She forced a light laugh. 'Look, we're just being paranoid. There must be thousands of cars like that.'

'So, we go back?'

'Yes.'

George drove along the main road, then turned once more into her street. A parking place had appeared outside her block, and he drew up into it. He glanced once more at the car across the road, then dismissed it from his mind.

'Are you rushing off?' Simone said.

'What do I have to rush off to?'

'Come on up, then.'

'You sure?'

She grinned at him, and opened her door. After he had locked the car she took his arm and led him to the main door. He watched while she opened the double lock.

As they waited for the lift to come to the ground floor she said: 'I thought you might have someone to rush off to.'

He gave her a surprised look.

'I thought you knew I hadn't.'

The lift arrived, and when they were inside Simone closed the criss-cross iron gates.

'Everyone should have.'

'You don't, Simone.'

'But I'm different.'

'I know.'

'I'm the girl other men rush home from.'

They were standing only inches apart, and George had never seen her as unguarded as this before.

He said: 'Don't you ever want someone, Simone?'

'Yes, of course I do. But like I told you, I'm different.'

'Not to me, you're not.'

The lift was whining upwards, lurching slightly on its elderly mountings. Simone tipped towards him, and he breathed her exotic fragrance. He raised a hand to touch her hair, and as he did so she looked up at him. Suddenly he realised how infrequently they had looked straight into each other's eyes.

The lift stopped, the moment held.

Simone said, very softly: 'Let's go.'

She pulled back the gate of the lift, and they stepped out into the landing.

Anderson was there.

Simone screamed. The black man moved towards them with animal ferocity, and terrifying speed. His arm swung from low down, like a rising punch, but his huge fist held the evil blade of an open razor. The fist slashed at Simone's face, aiming at her eyes.

George reacted without thinking. As Anderson swung at her, he dived in front of her, grabbing wildly for the man's arm, trying to deflect him. The man's strength was so great, though, that the cutting blow continued. The blade snicked past Simone's face, continued on, sliced viciously through George's forearm.

George howled with pain and fright, but he had hold of Anderson and the man was off-balance from the thrusting blow. George kicked instinctively at Anderson: the toe of his shoe against a shin, then a knee into the man's groin. Anderson barely flinched, and raised his deadly arm again. George threw a punch at his face, missed, caught him on the shoulder.

As Anderson swung around, George got free of him.

'*In the lift!*' he yelled . . . but Simone was already there.

George scrambled after her, slammed the iron gate closed and held it there as Anderson tried to force it open and snicked the razor through the bars. Simone hit the button, and the lift sank slowly down.

As they went down from the landing, they both saw Anderson move away . . . and heard his feet pounding on the concrete steps around them.

Blood was gushing from George's arm, and he held it to him in anguish.

'Oh Jesus . . . let me look at it,' Simone said.

'Ssh . . .'

The slow-moving lift had reached the landing below, and Anderson leapt into sight, roaring with rage and shaking at the gate.

Simone screamed again, and shrank back. George put his arm around her.

The lift went on slowly down. Somewhere around them, Anderson's feet raced down the steps.

He was there again at the next landing, waiting with his hand on the catch of the door, ready to snatch it open as the lift passed. George stood back, kicked at Anderson's hand.

The lift went on down. Anderson followed. They could hear him, they could feel him around them.

George said, quietly: 'Stop the lift.'

'Why?'

'Do it.'

They were between floors; Anderson was somewhere outside.

Simone jabbed desperately at the emergency stop button.

The lift car halted with an uneasy lurch.

Silence.

'Where is he?' Simone said.

George raised a finger to his lips, and whispered: 'Listen.'

They suddenly heard footsteps, but these were no longer the frantic pounding noises of a chase. Anderson was creeping somewhere behind them, on the stairs, or on one of the landings.

George crouched down slowly, holding his wounded arm against his chest; blood seeped into the front of his shirt. The floor of the lift car was just a few inches below the ceiling of the landing beneath them. Easing forward, George tried to peer out, but the view was too restricted. Anderson might be there, just a few inches away, out of sight, waiting with his hand on the catch of the door, ready to snatch it open as they passed.

Simone, huddled against the rear wall of the car, was trembling.

She mouthed at him: 'Is he there?'

George shook his head, trying to reassure her, but the fright was in him too and an uncontrollable tremor made his head tic to and fro twice more, shuddering.

His blood lay in streaks and pools all over the floor of the lift car.

Footsteps again. Soft, somewhere behind them.

George looked up.

Anderson was above them, visible through the upper few inches of the gate.

'*George!*'

He dived at the buttons, jabbed three of them at once. The elderly lift groaned, and started to sink once more.

But Anderson, crouching above them, hurled a small bottle with violent ease. It crashed into the car, and broke instantly on the wall beside Simone's head. She ducked away.

The vile smell of vitriol flooded around them.

George said urgently: 'Scream!'

'What?'

'Your eyes . . . he hit your eyes!'

Simone screamed, drew breath, screamed again.

The lift sank slowly. Outside, whenever Simone sucked in her breath, they could hear Anderson running again.

George, leaning against the gate, his hand resting on the buttons, watched the landings slip upwards past them. When they reached the halfway mark between the main entrance and the floor above, he hit the stop button. Anderson was moving somewhere above them.

George waited.

When he judged it right, he pressed the button to take the lift up again.

'Simone . . . *ssh*!'

She stopped her screaming, stood behind him, breathing with a desperate rasping noise.

George allowed the lift to rise to the halfway point just below Simone's floor, then stopped it again.

The building was silent, but they strained to hear.

George said, very quietly: 'Remind me. How far is it to your door?'

'Not far. Twenty yards.'

'Is there anywhere he could hide?'

'No.' She was staring at the bloodstained floor. 'I don't think so . . . no, there isn't.'

'Are you ready to try it?'

She shook her head.

'OK, then. Keep listening.'

They waited for five minutes, their nerves jangling, while George's blood seeped down his arm, into his clothes, dripped on the floor.

He said: 'Once more. OK?'

She nodded.

George hit one of the buttons, and the lift slowly sank. As they passed each landing they looked anxiously from side to side, while George stood ready to kick out at Anderson should he appear.

They went all the way to the bottom of the lift shaft, then rose again to Simone's floor. There was no sign of Anderson anywhere.

George let the lift stop on the landing, and he opened the gate cautiously. It was possible to see along the corridor in both directions; no one was there.

'You all right now?' he said to Simone.

'I think so.'

'He's not here. Come on.'

They stepped out of the bloodied lift, stinking of vitriol, and started along the corridor towards her door.

Another door opened, and a young woman came out. She slammed her door, then turned back to lock it.

George smiled and nodded to her. The woman glanced at him, saw the blood, looked away.

At Simone's door, while she found her keys, George said: 'You know some nice people.'

'Anderson?'

'Yes.'

'He's found out where I live, George. He knows where I *live*!'

'Come on, calm down.' She was fumbling with the keys, rattling them noisily against the lock. 'Let me do that.'

He took the keys from her, and when they were inside and the door was double locked, she held herself against him, shuddering and frightened. George's injured arm hung limply beside him, until the pressure made it throb with pain.

'You're good at this too,' George said.

'I'm good at most things.'

Once, George would have been alert for the double

meaning, or the snide undertone, but he had learnt that much of what Simone said about herself was literally true and could be taken that way. They were sitting on her couch, close together, feeling defensive of each other and close and united. He had his jacket off, and his torn shirtsleeve rolled up, and she was gently winding a bandage over the long slash.

Although it was unpleasant to look at, and still painful to bear, the wound was not deep; Anderson's razor had slit the skin and a shallow layer of flesh.

George's hand felt numb, but he had full use of it, and Simone's nursing was as expert as she said. When she finished, the arm was sore and stiff, but he knew that in a few days the worst would have healed up. That was something else he had always been able to do: mend quickly.

They felt secure for the time being. Once they were inside the flat they had searched it thoroughly, making sure that Anderson had not somehow found his way in, and also that he wouldn't be able to get in without making a *lot* of noise.

Simone had bounced back quickly. After cleaning George's wound, and putting a temporary dressing on it, she had taken a quick shower and changed her clothes. When she emerged she had recovered her poise; she fixed them both strong drinks, and finished off George's bandaging.

With immediate needs fulfilled now the problem remained of what to do next.

She recharged their glasses, but afterwards did not return to sit next to George. She went to the window, parted the curtains a fraction of an inch and peered down into the street.

'Is he out there?' George said.

'I can't see him.'

'What about the car?'

'I don't remember which one it was.'

George moved to her side.

'It's gone . . . if that was the one.'

'Then it was.' She raised both hands, clutched the fabric of the curtains, like a cat trying to climb them. 'Oh God! I'll never be safe again!'

George said, gloomily: 'The one thing that's sure, he'll be back.'

'What am I going to do?'

'Don't answer the doorbell.' He grinned wanly at her.

'Damn you, George.'

'The thing is, he can't get in. But he can get you any time he likes, whenever you go in and out.'

'I'd never thought of *that*,' she said, with heavy sarcasm. She moved away from him, prowling the room. She kept touching objects, as if sensing they were suddenly to be taken away from her; her life was changing, forced to change.

'We've got to get you out of here,' George said.

'I've nowhere to go . . . or nowhere that Anderson can't find me.'

'You could stay with me.'

She stared at him.

'You know, I don't even know where you live.' She said it as if it had been a revelation to her.

'Down by the river. With my mate Thomas. He likes detective books.'

'I don't like detective books.'

'You'd like Thomas.'

She shook her head. 'No . . . I'll get a room. Some-where anonymous.'

'Do you know somewhere?'

'The Westbury. They used to like me there.'

'What's that . . . a hotel?'

'Expensive. But I could pay my way.'

George stared at her.

'I've decided,' he said. 'What you're gonna do.'

'What?'

'Just this once. What I tell you to do.'

He pulled the car into the yard, then took Simone's bag from the back.

'What is this?' she said.

'My mate Thomas. He likes detective books.'

He led her through the workshop, and shoved open the door of the caravan.

'Don't you, Thomas?' he said out loud.

Sudden movement at the far end. George put a lighted match to one of the mantles, and in the soft glow they saw that Thomas was sitting bolt upright in his bunk, his eyes wide with surprise.

'Don't I what?' he said.

'I got something to tell you,' George said. 'The dwarf did it again.'

'What dwarf?' Simone said.

'The one that's been doing in the opera singers. Tell her, Thomas.'

Thomas levered himself out of the bunk, swinging his legs down so that he sat on the side. In the process, he revealed that he slept in a pair of underpants that looked extremely evil.

'Well,' he said. 'There's this dwarf, see, and a

whole lot of opera singers. Now, there's a kind of horse called a Percheron, and –'

'A what?' said Simone.

'A Percheron. A sort of carthorse, all black. All right, now the important thing about this horse is –'

'Thomas,' George said.

'They keep finding it, see –'

'Thomas,' George said.

'– and . . . what?'

'You haven't been introduced. Thomas, this is Simone. Simone, Thomas.'

'Great. So these opera singers keep being bumped off, you see, and –'

George said: 'He'll go on like this all night.'

'Where am I going to sleep?' said Simone.

Chapter 21

George waited until he was *sure*. Being sure was a feeling he knew, one that had got him through bad times in the old days. It wasn't the same as being certain about something; it was nothing to do with finding out facts. *Sure*ness was for him an inner thing, a growing sense of conviction that he felt the way he did, that he had to do something, and that what he planned to do was going to be right.

It had never let him down. When George was *sure*, he never went wrong.

He had been brooding too long about Mortwell and Anderson and Cathy, and the whole damned thing. It was time to act, but first he had to be sure.

Then he was, and it was like a feeling of clear-headedness: a dousing in cold water, an awakening to reality after a disturbing dream. He could taste it, smell it; his body urged for action. He had not felt like this since before he went inside.

With this grew a second new quality. His instinct for trouble, and the way to deal with it, overcame the lesser instincts, to stay out of trouble, to accept his role of kickstand for other people. Suddenly, as if inspired, he knew what to do . . . and, more important, he knew who to do it to.

He left Thomas' place in a quiet mood, and drove

slowly across the river towards the Blackheath area of South London. Beside him, on the passenger seat, and concealed inside an ordinary paper bag, was the Walther PPK that Thomas had obtained for him. George had an abiding distrust of guns, but an equally abiding respect for their usefulness.

Sometimes, there was no alternative to the form of self-defence they undoubtedly provided. There was no longer any doubt in George's mind what would happen to him if he met Anderson again.

Or Mortwell.

Mortwell was the man. Anderson did the work, but Mortwell was the man.

In his new lucidity, George drove across the heath and through the surrounding sidestreets without pausing to check with the streetmap. It was years since he had been here, but he found the way as if it had been only yesterday.

He also remembered the trick of parking. Mortwell had shown him once. 'Don't go near the house, Georgie,' he had said. 'Much better to stay out of sight. Little lane, around the back.' Mortwell had never liked George making his presence known in Blackheath.

The little lane was still there: a pathway, really, used by people who rode horses or who went jogging. It was easy to park there, under trees, surrounded by bushes, invisible from the house. And twenty yards away there was access to the road: a quick left turn, another to the right, and he would be on a fast dual carriageway to the south.

Very convenient. It was no wonder that the part of the lane by Mortwell's house had tyre tracks all over it. George was not the only one who used it. A lot of people who visited Dinny liked to make a fast getaway afterwards.

George was therefore unsurprised to discover that another car was already there, a large grey Mercedes, guiltily hidden under trees and amid bushes. He stopped the Jaguar in front of it, deliberately blocking it in.

George checked his gun. He released the box magazine, and made sure the firing mechanism was working, then returned the clip to its place. Thomas had told him it was almost new, barely used. It wouldn't jam . . . but he had to watch the recoil. 'Use both hands and aim low,' he had said. 'Go for the goolies, and you'll smash the chest.'

'Where do you learn all this?' George had said, then added: 'Don't tell me . . . out of books.'

But Thomas disapproved of guns.

George slipped the Walther into an inner pocket, one he had enlarged and strengthened deliberately. The safety catch was on.

He walked to the wooden gate that opened into the grounds of Mortwell's house, climbed over it, then strolled calmly down through the undergrowth and trees until he could see the house. The time was late afternoon, and the autumnal sunshine was touching the roof.

It was the sort of place coveted by stockbrokers, merchant bankers and petty gangsters alike: a sumptuous redbrick Edwardian villa, with towers and gables and mullioned windows. Two small wings jutted from the main building, creating a pleasant patio between. Looking at the place with narrowed eyes, or sheer naïveté, it gave every impression of class and good taste. But all that was just a front, Mortwell's way of finding an incognito. George had vivid memories of what used to go on inside, and, for all he knew, still did.

He found a convenient place to wait, and sat down with his legs crossed. A clump of untended brambles spread in front of him, giving him cover, but allowing him a clear view of the house.

A few minutes passed before he saw movement. A light came on in the room that opened on to the patio, and Mortwell appeared inside. He stepped to the windows and drew the curtains, and then apparently returned to switch off the light.

After a few seconds George saw the curtains moving, and the French window that led to the patio was opened. Mortwell came outside, and closed the French window behind him.

He stood on the patio for a few seconds, glancing in an unworried away around the garden. He was wearing an evening suit with bow tie. As George watched he reached inside the suit jacket, withdrew a large cigar, snipped off the end and lit it.

He drew several times on the cigar, puffing out the smoke, enjoying himself. Then, with one hand slipped comfortably into the jacket pocket, the other holding the cigar, Mortwell walked leisurely towards one of the wings of the house. There was a second door here; Mortwell took a ring of keys from his pocket, let himself in and closed the door behind him.

George waited for another minute or two, the clarity of his intentions undiminished. He left his hiding place and walked coolly across the wide lawn. He was aware that if anyone were looking from the house he would be seen, but he was trusting to his luck.

It was to do with being sure; it was also something to do with the gun in his pocket.

The French window was unlocked, and George slipped quietly through it. The space beyond was one that in any other house of this sort might be used as a pleasant breakfast room, or some kind of conservatory . . . but in Mortwell's house had been converted to other, more sinister purposes. George knew this room from the old days. He had even been in it once, at Mortwell's invitation. The family; Mortwell always wanted his damned family around him.

Across the opposite wall was a pair of thick velvet curtains, and facing these were several easy chairs. A large video camera was mounted on a tripod, pointing towards the curtains, and several movie cameras lay carelessly in a heap on a shelf at the side. Pausing long enough to make absolutely sure there was no one else present, George walked across to the curtains and snatched them open.

Bright light poured in on him through the glass wall that was there.

This was the setup Mortwell jokingly referred to as his amusement arcade. The area beyond the glass was fitted out as a sexual fantasy room: a huge bed, a bath, several long tables with padded tops . . . all arranged so they were in clear view of this place and the cameras it contained. Mortwell had equipped the room with every possible aid to sexual gratification; George knew that all kinds of fetishistic clothes and underwear were to be found in the closets, and hanging on racks along the walls was a wide assortment of perverted sexual instruments: whips and thongs and chains and ropes, leather masks and short rubber truncheons, vibrators and dildos. The ceiling was mirrored, and so were large areas of wall; this wall, the one that backed on to the small auditorium, was of course equipped with a two-way mirror.

All this George had seen before.

What he was not prepared to see were the two people present in the room.

Cathy was there, and she was with a client.

The man was middle-aged, overweight and balding. He was naked, and in a state of high sexual excitement. He had Cathy in his arms: not caressing her, but manhandling her. She was dressed in a simple white shift, loose and waistless, semi-transparent. The man was holding her from behind, his arms wrapped around her stomach, bending her forward.

As George watched, the man forced her towards him, right up to the two-way mirror, and thrust her against it. Her face warped and distorted as she was pressed against the glass. The man pushed her head down, so that she was crouching, and the pale skin of her young face abraded against the smooth glass. When he had moved her to the position he wanted her in the man pulled up the shift and threw it over her back and head, then snatched the girl's briefs down her legs.

He entered her forcefully from behind, jerking and thrusting.

George stared in horror, all his earlier calmness swept away by this sight. What he saw, and what he could not stop seeing, was Cathy's face. It was like that of a dead girl. Her eyes were glazed, her mouth was slack. She seemed hardly to be breathing; her arms hung limply at her side. She appeared to be barely conscious, totally at the mercy of the man.

His violent pleasure was as brief as it was brutal. He soon withdrew from her, stepping back, leaving her at the mirror. She stayed in the position the man had placed her in: semiconscious, slumped against the unyielding glass.

The man moved across the room to one of the padded tables, and here for the first time George noticed that two or three flat dishes had been arranged. There was a glint of colour: it looked to him as if the dishes contained sweets.

Or capsules of drugs.

When the man picked up a hypodermic syringe, and started screwing a phial into it, George knew beyond doubt what the man was engaged in doing. The man, standing with his back to the girl at the mirror, raised the syringe to the light and squirted a thin jet of liquid into the air.

George came to an impulsive decision, and acted on it. There was a door at the side of the two-way mirror, concealed from those inside the room, and Cathy was already partially leaning against it. George opened this door, and the girl slumped into his arms.

The man was speaking into the air, a torrent of vile promises: '. . . I'll fill your cunt with shit, put piss in your mouth, fill you with –'

George pulled Cathy into the anteroom, and quietly closed the door. In the room, the man continued with his disgusting litany, turning at last to where he thought the girl should be.

In the anteroom George said, quietly and urgently: 'Are you awake?'

' 'Course I am.' The girl faced him, but her eyelids were drooping, and her head would not stay erect.

'Can you walk?'

'If you help me.' Cathy's words were slurred, and her attention seemed always to be wandering. 'Who are you?'

'Never mind that. Get your knickers on.'

The flimsy garment was still tangled around her ankles, and with confused movements the girl bent down to pull them up. She straightened the shift around her body, using the flat of her hand as if trying to rub off something that was sticking to the palm.

Inside the room, George saw that the man had hurriedly pulled on some clothes, had opened the door and was shouting to someone outside.

'Come on,' George said to the girl. 'Mortwell's going to be looking for you.'

He ushered her across to the French window, pushed her through in front of him, then grabbed her arm and ran her across the lawn, tugging at her arm. Cathy, barefoot and weak, kept stumbling, and weaving from side to side.

'I've seen you,' she said suddenly.

'Shut up, and keep running!'

'What you doing here?'

'I'm from Simone. Remember Simone?'

The girl tripped, and George had to haul her to her feet. Behind them, Mortwell had appeared on the patio.

He shouted: 'George! What the *fuck* . . .?'

'Come on, Cathy!' George yelled, pulling desperately at her arm. They were now in the tangle of trees, and when George looked back he could no longer see Mortwell.

They reached the car. George bundled the girl into the passenger seat, slammed the door on her, and ran around to the driver's side.

The engine fired on the first attempt, and without preamble George threw it into gear and accelerated away, kicking up a shower of soil and dead leaves behind him.

Mortwell appeared in the lane behind them, panting and coughing. He stood there long enough to note the car, then turned and walked quickly back to his house.

Chapter 22

Certain they were being followed, George drove as fast as he thought he could without attracting the unwelcome attentions of the police.

When they were clear of London, he swung abruptly into a country lane, drove quickly through two villages, then pulled over and parked in the entrance to a field to wait to see what would happen. When no other cars came along, he carried on through the back roads until he found the main highway further along, then drove at a less frenetic speed. Throughout all this, Cathy sat in silence in the passenger seat beside him. She was less than good company. For a lot of the time she lolled back in the seat with her eyes closed, her head swinging gently from side to side. Her mouth was slack and her lips were wet, and her hands rested limply in her lap. When she was not dozing she fretted in the seat, fidgeting with the seat belt and the adjustable back. At times like this she seemed manic and over-active, supercharged with an unnatural energy. Then she would suddenly slump again, her eyes either closed or staring listlessly into space.

She answered none of George's questions, and after a while he gave up trying to make conversation.

Cathy was pretty in a fey way, her features looking

innocent and childlike when she was in repose. Her clothes, too, gave the same impression: the simple shift dress would have looked well on a twelve-year old. But the appearance was a deception. There were tired lines around her eyes, and the nails on her hands were broken and bitten back. Her knuckles were coarse-skinned, and her flesh had an unhealthy pallor. And the dress: it was thin and loose-fitting, and provocatively translucent. George already knew that she was virtually naked beneath it, because he had seen her in the room, but even if he had not known he would have been left in little doubt. As she shifted in the seat beside him, turning from side to side, the loose folds of the front often fell open to reveal her breasts, and the skirt rode up to show most of her white thighs.

Even semi-conscious, she had the natural talent of arousing male interest, and George was not immune from it.

Once they were back on the main road, she became temporarily more alert: she sat up in the seat, looked around at the passing countryside, then glanced at George.

'Is this what you do for a living?' she said. Her voice had that deceptively calm quality of the drugged.

'What? Driving around?'

'You know . . . breaking into houses.'

'Only when I'm going to kick a pervert,' George said, still feeling pleased about the ease with which he had been able to spring the girl from Mortwell's house.

'He's going to come for me,' Cathy said.

'Who? Mortwell?' George took his eyes from the road to look at her, and registered that fear lay behind the bland, dozy eyes. 'Nah.'

'How can you be so sure?'

'Just believe me, would you?'

She started to cry then, bending her head so that the tears fell lightly on to her dress. She sniffed a couple of times, so George reached behind him and pulled forward a box of Kleenex from the back seat. She blew her nose, then tossed the crumpled tissue out of the window.

'Anderson,' she said.

'What about him?'

'He's going to kill me. You too.'

'Not if he can't find us, he isn't.'

She looked back over her shoulder at the road behind, making George glance quickly into the rear-view mirror. There was nothing behind them, though, or at least there was no car that seemed likely to be Mortwell's, or any of the others.

'Can't you drive faster?' she said.

'Can't you relax a bit?'

She stayed alert for a few more minutes, but then the drugs took her again and she subsided into her half-waking state. George drove on.

A few miles outside Brighton he slowed the car, signalled left, then drove into the car park of a road-side café. Very few cars were already there.

George got out and looked around. The South Downs rose behind the café, and a cool wind funnelled along the valley.

Inside the car, Cathy was stirring. George went back to her.

She said: 'I'm hungry.'

'Yeah, but we got to wait here.'

'Why?'

'Because I say so.'

'Where's Simone? You said Simone had sent you.'

'I don't know where she is,' he said truthfully.

'I want something to eat.'

She opened the car door and stepped out. The loose gravel of the yard bit into her naked feet, and she staggered slightly. George caught her arm to support her, and as he did so her loose-fitting dress slipped down from one shoulder and bared most of her breast.

George hastily moved the dress back into place.

'Look, if you want to go in there, you got to quit falling out of your dress. Can't you button it up, or something?'

'Could do.' She grinned at him, but it was a forced rictus, a sudden lapse into professional technique. 'You want to do it with me?'

'Are you *kidding*?'

'That's the idea, isn't it? That's why you took me?'

'Do up your dress, Cathy.'

'OK.' She picked at the buttons with her fingers, but the act of lowering her head caused her to lose balance once again, and she took a step to one side to stop herself falling.

'What was that bastard pumping into you?' George said.

'Nothing much.'

'Do you know what it was?'

She shook her head vaguely. 'I liked it.'

'Come on, let's get a cup of tea.'

He led her into the diner, and they went to a booth by the window that overlooked the car park. Cathy slumped in her seat, draping her thin arms across the tabletop and playing idly with the sugar in the bowl. George stared at the tattoo on the back of her hand.

He said: 'Why did you put that on your hand?'

She raised her arm, squinted at the tattoo, then smiled.

'Because of Simone.'

'You did it together?'

'No . . . just me.' She traced the inner heart with a fingertip, then the outer one. 'This is me, this is her.'

The waitress came to the table, holding a small order-pad.

'Can I take your order?' she said.

'Yeah . . . I'll have steak and chips, and a cup of tea, please. What about you?' he said to Cathy.

'Ice cream.'

'I thought you wanted to eat something.'

'Ice cream.'

'All right.' George nodded to the waitress, who scribbled the order on the pad, then went away. George said: 'You just want ice cream.'

'It's the only thing I can eat.'

'What do you mean?'

'You know.'

'I don't bloody know,' he said, remembering May, and the last time he had been in a café with a child whore.

'Can't take food any more. Not real food.'

'What can you take?'

She looked at him critically, frowning. 'You don't know anything, do you?'

'No . . . I don't know anything.'

169

The waitress returned with the ice cream, and Cathy immediately picked up a spoon and started eating it.

'I don't mean to be rude,' she said with her mouth full. 'I like you, you know.'

'I'm glad.'

'Do you like me?'

'I don't know you, do I?'

Cathy stared silently at her empty ice cream bowl as George finished his meal and then drank his tea. People were staring at her, especially the men, and he felt, just as he had done with May, that people would be thinking of him as the father. In some ways he wished Cathy *was* his daughter: she wouldn't be in this state if she had been.

And so, once again, he slipped into thinking about Jeanie, full of regrets.

They were both roused from their individual reveries by the arrival of a car, crunching over the gravel outside. Thomas was at the wheel.

Glancing at Cathy, George saw that she had noticed Simone.

He said: 'Wait there.'

He went outside quickly, and was there in time to open the passenger door for Simone.

'Hello,' George said.

She ignored him, brushed past him and hurried into the café.

Thomas climbed out, and leaned against the side of the car.

'You like her, don't you?' he said.

'Do you?'

'Don't know her, do I?'

Simone and Cathy were together, illuminated by the bright lights inside the building. George saw Simone lean over Cathy, wrapping her arms around the girl's neck and shoulders, fondling her hair and pressing her face to her chest. Cathy seemed in more of a stupor than ever before, and was staring dumbly at the tabletop.

Simone stared out at George.

Thomas said: 'Not a very good bet, though, are you?'

'No . . . no, I'm not.'

'What's the story, George?'

'It's complicated.'

'More complicated than *The Deadly Percheron*?'

'Much more.'

'What about these two, then?' Thomas said, nodding towards Simone and Cathy.

'You tell me. I just did what I was asked.'

'You never learn, do you?' said Thomas.

'I do . . . all the time.'

Chapter 23

George drove slowly down the front at Brighton, weaving through the heavy traffic. It was dark, and he was feeling he had had a long day.

Simone and Cathy were in the back of the Jaguar. Cathy was asleep in Simone's arms.

'Are you looking for somewhere particular to go?' he said over his shoulder.

'Not really.'

'Then what are we doing?'

'Driving around. I thought you knew.'

'You want to do this all night?'

A long silence followed, and George tipped the rear-view mirror to see what was happening. Nothing was happening: Simone was staring out of a side window towards the sea.

At last she said: 'We'll go to a hotel.'

'Thank the Lord for that. Which one?'

'Any you like. Pick one at random.'

'What . . . big, small? Posh? Cheap?'

'That one there.' Simone pointed to one on the town side of the road.

'Posh,' George muttered under his breath as he swung the car across the central reservation and bumped up the ramp to the unloading bay. Here a snooty commissionaire told him he would have to move the car to the underground park. Simone roused Cathy, and helped her in through the main door.

Several minutes later, George went into the reception area of the hotel, and, rather to his surprise, found Simone and Cathy waiting for him. The girl was now looking very much the worse for wear, and Simone said she could not support her weight much longer.

'I'll take her,' George said. 'You bring the luggage.'

'Luggage?' Simone said.

'Ah,' said George. 'Joke.'

He slipped an arm around Cathy's waist, and draped one of her own arms around his neck. Under the curious gaze of the hotel staff, he tugged her across to the lift.

Simone had taken two rooms adjacent to each other: a single and a double. She opened the door of the double, and George dragged Cathy in and across to the bed.

Her eyes opened briefly.

'Where is she?' she said, indistinctly.

'Who?'

In the same moment, Simone said: 'I'm here.'

Cathy turned her head, and looked blearily across to Simone.

'Who is this, Simone?'

'This is George. He's –'

'I know. He's the ice cream man. Mr Whippy. Is your van outside, Mr Whippy?'

She started to laugh, a high, hysterical giggling, devoid of any humour. She hiccoughed and choked, and snorted messily through her nose.

'Jesus! We've got to do something about her!'

173

Simone rushed into the bathroom, came back with some tissues and began to clean the girl up. Cathy lay back on the bed, still giggling insensibly.

George picked up one of her hands, which was trailing down towards the floor. He folded it over her chest.

'She's burning hot,' he said.

'I know.' Simone placed her palm on Cathy's forehead. 'They've given her a habit. God alone knows what it is.'

'I can guess,' George said.

Cathy was fretting on the bed, struggling as if against invisible bonds. Simone held her down, pressing on both shoulders to restrain her.

'Shouldn't we get a doctor?'

Simone scowled at him. 'There'll be a chemist open somewhere. There always is in Brighton. Do me a favour, would you?'

'What?'

Simone released Cathy for a few moments, and reached across to the bedside table for the folder of hotel notepaper. She scribbled something on a sheet, and passed it to George.

'Go and get this, would you?'

'What is it . . . a prescription?'

'The pharmacist will know what it is.'

'I can't read it. You're not a doctor too, are you?'

'You'd better hurry.'

He had rarely seen her looking so serious. He turned to the door, opened it, and then had second thoughts.

'Simone . . . there's something you'd better have.'

'What?'

'Just in case.' He reached into his pocket, and brought out the gun. 'Never know, do you?'

She took it from him, balanced it in her hand. She still looked serious.

'Do you think Mortwell can find us? Or Anderson?'

'They found where you live.'

She bent her head, looking first at the gun, then at the helpless girl on the bed beside her.

'Do you know how to use it?' George said.

'Go get the medicine.'

As George left she was slipping the gun under the spare pillow on the bed.

It took George more than an hour to get back to the hotel; the only chemist open was a long way from the seafront, close to the railway station. The assistant gave him the drugs after an inaudible conversation with the duty pharmacist.

She said: 'Do you know how to administer this correctly?'

'Yeah . . . 'course I do.'

He walked quickly back to the hotel, keeping a watchful eye for anyone he did not want to see. Everything seemed normal: Brighton was at the end of its holiday season, but there were still many people thronging the streets. George liked Brighton; he remembered a job he had done for Mortwell here, back in the old days.

He took the lift up to the floor below the rooms, just in case he was being followed . . . an old trick, but still a useful one. He went the remainder of the way up the emergency stairs, hidden at the far end of the corridor.

He let himself into the room, expecting Simone to be angry about the amount of time he had taken.

Instead, a tableau of calm. . .

The room was almost dark, the only light coming from the small lamp just inside the door. Simone and Cathy were together on the bed.

Simone had removed all of Cathy's clothes, and tossed them on the floor. She herself had stripped down to just her briefs. She lay beside the girl, one hand delving deep into the softness between Cathy's legs, the other beneath her head, supporting her gently. Simone was lying across the girl, kissing gently on one of her nipples.

Cathy was asleep . . . or unconscious.

Simone did not move away, although she must have heard George walk in.

Finally, he said: 'I brought the medicine.' Simone made no acknowledgement of him. He added: 'I'll leave it here for you.'

'Thank you, George,' she said indistinctly. Then she raised her face, and looked at him. 'The single room is for you.'

'I'd guessed,' he said, angrily.

Chapter 24

George watched television for a couple of hours, then became restless and went outside. He found a pub in The Lanes, and stayed there until closing time, drinking quickly, determined to get drunk. But he still felt sober as he walked back to the hotel, and he knew that if he went up to the room he would lie there in brooding wakefulness.

He walked down to the beach, and clattered across the shingle to the sea's edge. Here he turned his back on the waves and looked back towards the town: he saw the lights from streetlamps, windows and signs, and the moving brilliance of traffic, but the sea sucked up all the noise from the town so that it seemed to exist in frigid silence.

He turned again and pissed on the shingle, watching the luminescence of the waves as they broke and roared towards him.

It was the first time he had seen the sea since leaving prison, and here he was pissing into it. George grinned sardonically into the night, thinking of Simone and Cathy.

He strolled along the beach for a while until he reached the great metal legs of one of the piers. He stood beneath the walkway, looking up at the dark shape above, peering along its length, out to sea, the pier black against the moonlit water. Barnacles crusted the metal legs, and old seaweed made them slimy to the touch.

George remembered the job he had done for Mortwell in Brighton several years before. Mortwell always fancied himself as a stylist, an eccentric. He had brought George and the others on to one of these piers, encouraged them to go on the Dodgem cars, shoot pennies into the games in the arcade, wear seaside hats. Five petty criminals, out on a job, pretending to be having a good time just so Mortwell could play at being a father figure.

That night, in Brighton, a watchman had been shot during the raid. He didn't die, and Mortwell and George and the others had got away with it, but it made Brighton too hot for a long time.

George wondered if Simone had known this when she fled to Brighton to elude Mortwell's network of pimps.

Anderson . . .

Where had Anderson come from? He was new to Mortwell's lot, so he must have come along in the last seven years. Way back then, Mortwell's interest in vice had been a sideline. If there had been pimps at that time George didn't know of them, and he reckoned that someone like Anderson would not have commanded the eminence he now seemed to have with Mortwell.

Walking back up the beach George remembered how Mortwell had tried to set him up for the shooting in Brighton. That was the first time, and he had had the wit to see it coming. Not the second, when he took the rap.

That was much of George's resentment against Mortwell, that he had been taken for a mug.

Now he was wondering if it was happening again. There was a basic contradiction, and it had been nagging away at the back of his mind.

Simone had said that Anderson did not know where she lived, and her realisation that he had found her seemed genuinely horrified.

Yet Anderson worked for Mortwell, or perhaps even vice versa. Anyway, they worked together. Dudley and Terry *did* work for Mortwell; they always had, and they were still at it. Dudley had got him the driving job, the stuff with the auto-pager . . . and through the driving job he had met Simone. If Dudley knew Simone, then Mortwell knew Simone . . . and Anderson always had, back when he was her pimp.

Coincidence?

Or had Anderson known where Simone was all along? Was he, George, being set up for a mug once again?

The more he thought about it the less he liked it, and sensed trouble brewing. Big trouble, probably for himself.

Meanwhile Simone, the only person in all this that he really cared about, lay up in that room playing finger pie with a bombed-out teenage whore.

Feeling disagreeable, and as wide awake as ever before, George let himself into his room. Although he pressed his ear to the connecting wall, he could hear nothing from next door.

179

Chapter 25

He slept fitfully, but must in the end have fallen into deep sleep. It was broad daylight when he was woken by a knock on the door. The sun was glancing in and reflecting off the mirror over the convenience table.

The knocking came again at the door.

'A minute,' he shouted, and shuffled into his trousers. Expecting it to be a chambermaid, he opened the door.

It was Simone. She was fully dressed, and had her bag over her shoulder.

'You going to invite me in?' she said.

'You want to come in?'

He closed the door behind her.

'What's doing?' he said.

'It's a nice day. I thought we could go for a walk on the front.'

'We got some talking to do.'

'Good. We can do it while we walk.'

He rubbed a hand over his bristly chin. 'I'm not exactly ready to go out. What about a cup of tea first?'

'We'll find somewhere.'

She sat down to wait for him.

'You walk in here cool as a cucumber,' George said. 'What about . . . you know?' He jerked a thumb towards the next room.

'Cathy? She's asleep.'

'Been up all night, have you?'

'She's very ill, George.'

'That's what you were doing, right? Kiss of life, and all that.'

Simone said nothing, but stared through the window at the traffic, and the sea beyond.

'Well, I'm going to have a shave.'

Twenty minutes later they were strolling along the promenade in the warm sunshine. The weather had brought out the crowds, even so late in the season. People were sitting on the beach; a few had ventured into the water. George peered over the rail, hoping to see a fat lady in a red bathing costume, but on the shingle immediately beneath the promenade two young girls had spread out towels and were sunbathing. They were both topless.

'Here, look at that!' George said, and Simone looked down.

'It's nothing special,' she said. 'You see that everywhere on beaches now.'

'How long's that been going on?'

'How long were you inside?' she replied, walking on.

After one more interested look, George followed her. As they walked along he noticed several more semi-naked girls, and decided that some things had changed for the better.

A little later he said: 'You done a lot of this, haven't you?'

'What?'

'Walking along here.'

'It's what people do at the seaside.'

'So you've done this before?'

'Every day.'

'With your gentleman friends?'

'Sometimes.'

'Show me the sights, then.'

'You getting at something?' Simone said.

If he was, it was general in nature. George's mood was deteriorating fast, a counterpoint to the overall atmosphere of harmless gaiety being radiated by everyone else he could see. The simple pleasures of a seaside walk on a sunny day were too straightforward to deal with the complex rage that was in him. George scowled at the ground.

They had reached the part of the promenade that opened on to one of the piers, and Simone paused.

'Shall we go on the pier?' she said.

'That part of your regular beat too?'

'I've been on it before, if that's what you mean.'

George made an attempt to rally his spirits.

'Come on, then,' he said. 'Let's sample the old briny.'

He tossed some coins at the woman behind the turnstile, and they set off along the ancient wooden walkway leading out over the sea. A short way along, George saw a stall selling cheap sunglasses, and he led Simone over. Still making his expansive gesture, trying to conceal the deep bitterness inside him, he grabbed at the first two pairs he saw.

'Here you are, guv,' he said to the vendor, and pressed a five-pound note into his hand. It was far too much, but George was too preoccupied to worry about a little thing like that.

'Put these on,' he said, handing one of the pairs to Simone.

'I don't like them,' she said.

The smoked lenses were contained in plastic frames shaped like two red hearts. His own pair were blue, with ridiculous spikes prodding out from the frames.

'Go on, wear them,' he said. He put on his own, having to force them into place. His forehead was too wide, or his ears were too far back, or something. Simone's fitted her more easily.

'You should see yourself,' she said.

'You're right. I *am* cheap.'

He stepped away from her, and she trotted to keep up with him.

George glanced up at the sun.

'Seven years . . . that's how long. I could do with a suntan.'

'What's got into you today?'

He ignored the question.

'Come on, Simone, show me the sights. Get me some Brighton rock . . . or buy me some candyfloss. Let's get in the right mood. We're on our holidays, aren't we? We're meant to have fun. You know the way it is. Men and women . . . they have fun, they link arms, have a cuddle, maybe he even kisses her. They love each other, and they get married so they can love each other a little better. They have a little baby. Only a little one, though. He fights with the fucking mother-in-law, you know. Men and fucking women . . . even mothers-in-law are fucking women. So she starts screwing around with other men, and he gets a bit in too . . . nothing serious, just a bit on the side. And then they both find out, and they cut it out and start fucking each other again, and the next thing they have another little baby –'

Simone wrenched herself away from him, and went to stand at the rail, staring down at the sea.

'So . . . ?' George said.

'So what?'

'Say something, damn you! Anything!'

'About what?'

'What I just said. Or last night.'

Simone frowned, and looked away.

'I'm sorry,' she said. 'I can't. I'm –'

'You're worried.'

'Yes.'

'So will you tell me?' George said.

'Tell you what?'

He took a breath. 'As my good mate Thomas would say, the whole story.'

'Trouble with your mate Thomas is he only thinks in stories. Not everyone has got one.'

There was a group of entertainers on the pier, and they started busking behind them. A man with a concertina started a simple, repetitive melody, a woman chanted words they could not make out, and a dwarf began dancing ingeniously. George turned to look.

Then he said: 'You like her, don't you?'

'Of course I like her.'

'But you like her that special way . . . the way they sing in songs.'

'What songs?' Simone said.

'Love songs. ". . . and I sold myself for a pair of dykes".'

Anger flickered across Simone's face.

'She *needs* me, George.'

'And you needed me to find her for you.'

'Didn't you ever need someone?'

'All the time.'

She yielded nothing: her face had a cold, stony look, and George knew that he had lost her from the moment he found Cathy. They were hidden away behind some barrier of womanly love, one he could never penetrate.

He said: 'I guess that's it, then.'

'Do you think it doesn't hurt?'

'Do you?'

'Let's leave it at that.'

He turned away from her, rested his elbows on the rail of the pier and stared blankly at the water. A speedboat was dashing ridiculously around, throwing white foam in the air.

He heard the clicking of Simone's high heels as she walked slowly away from him.

The spikes on his sunglasses were pricking into the upper slope of his cheeks, so he eased their position.

'George!'

He blinked, and stared at the sea. It was over.

'For God's sake! *George!*'

He turned then. Simone was ten yards away from him, facing him, half-crouched in the urgency of horror. Behind her, pushing violently through the crowds on the pier, three men were running towards her.

Two of them were Dudley and Terry. Anderson was in the lead, and he had a hand reaching into an inner pocket of his jacket, ready to use whatever was there.

Chapter 26

George had a moment of clarity, an instantaneous flash of perception. The pier at this point was divided along the centre by a double row of wooden seats, protected and separated by an ornate canopy built of wrought iron. To his right, the amusement building with the slot machines loomed up, and the space between this and the end of the canopy was where the dwarf and the others were busking. Simone stood to his left, frozen in horror, and Anderson and the others were rushing up behind her.

There was only one way to escape, and that was past the amusement building . . . either to dash around to the other side of the canopy and hope to run back to land, or to follow the pier further out to sea, along the more narrow platforms that ran along each side of the arcade. Neither possibility seemed to offer much hope: the three men were almost on them.

George reached into his pocket for the gun . . . then remembered he had given it to Simone, and she had placed it under the pillow.

All this took around a second to sink in, before George started moving.

He yelled: '*Run, damn you!*' Simone seemed paralysed in place. She was looking towards Anderson and the others, still partly huddled in fear. 'Come *on*, Simone!' George shouted at her.

He seized her arm and spun her around, and dragged her up the pier towards the amusement building. Now he had acted, Simone moved quickly. They ran together to the end of the canopy and skittered around it, Simone wobbling dangerously on her high heels. As they rounded the corner, they discovered that the buskers had changed position: George barged into the man with the concertina, knocking him to one side, and Simone collided with the dwarf, who was now performing agile acrobatic tricks. Simone tripped, and the dwarf fell to the floor. George snatched at Simone's arm, pulled her to her feet and made her keep running.

Anderson was a few feet behind them. He paused, looked back and shouted something.

Then he set off after them again.

Looking to the side, through the open canopy, George saw Terry and Dudley running parallel to them, intending to cut them off where the walkway broadened out further along. With Simone's arm still firmly grasped in his hand, George put on a spurt. Simone shouted that she couldn't run in these shoes, but the same urgency was in her.

Any chance of escape was hopeless. The pier was too crowded, and there were two of them, clinging to each other, running and weaving through the people . . . while Anderson was fit and strong and on his own, gaining on them with terrifying ease. Terry and Dudley had already outstripped them, and were somewhere ahead.

'*Keep going!*' George shouted, and released her arm.

He had spotted a wheeled flower stall tucked under

the canopy, and he dived to the side, knocking the flower-seller out of the way. As he turned he saw Anderson was almost on him. He grabbed the handles of the stall, tried to roll it . . . but it was too heavy, and all he could manage was to spin it around.

It was just enough. The corner of it crashed into Anderson's hip, deflecting him. Anderson staggered, momentarily off-balance, and his hand came out of the jacket holding the cutthroat razor.

George scooped his arm along the stall, hurling bundles of flowers at the man. As Anderson ducked, moving in, George leapt past him.

Anderson faced him, balancing athletically, both arms spread, the razor ready.

George feinted to the side, but Anderson knew every trick. He accepted the feint, raised his razor hand, and came in for the cut. The blade flashed towards George's neck.

George kicked out as violently as he could, the only defence left to him.

He was lucky. His foot slammed into Anderson's groin with instant effect. The man gasped and crumpled; the razor missed, fell from his hand and clattered across the wooden walkway.

George realised that people were screaming. As he backed away from Anderson's doubled body, he glanced wild-eyed at the small crowd that had witnessed the fight. Men had arms protectively around their women, and as George stepped away from Anderson they all backed off nervously.

He saw the razor on the floor, kicked at it . . . and it skidded across the boards and fell over the side into the sea.

Anderson was getting to his feet, his face distorted by rage and pain.

George ran off, following Simone. He saw her almost at once: she had been caught by Dudley and Terry, held by her arms. With the fear of Anderson still dominant, George was electric with adrenalin. He went straight up to Dudley, who was the nearer, and without preamble clouted his fist against the man's temple. Dudley fell to the side, releasing Simone.

'Fuck off, George!' Terry said. 'We've no argument with you.'

'But I have with you.'

George raised his fist and moved in . . . but Terry instantly let go of Simone's arm and moved back. He raised a defensive hand.

'OK, George . . . OK.'

George said: 'Come on, Simone!'

They ran again, shoving their way through the crowds.

They had to slow down to get through the exit turnstile. George pushed Simone ahead of him, and looked back.

The three men had regrouped. Anderson was talking to the other two, standing erect with his hands on his hips, flexing his back, like an athlete at the end of a race. Dudley looked cowed, and was standing with his shoulders hunched, pressing his hand to the side of his head.

Terry was pointing in their direction.

As George watched, the three of them began walking towards them.

Outside the pier, panting heavily, Simone said: 'What do we *do*?'

189

'We get to the car and drive like fuck.'

'No! We've got to take Cathy with us!'

'The hell with her . . . she's safe where she is.'

'George, they've *found* us. We can't leave her!'

'But if we go back to the hotel they're going to follow us.'

Even so, they had both started walking quickly in the direction of the hotel.

Looking back again, George saw that the three men were following them at a distance, making no attempt to catch them up or intercept them.

George was as out of breath as Simone, and now the brief fight was over he felt simultaneously drained and ready for more trouble. He was thinking of the gun, stashed away under the pillow . . .

'We'll make it difficult for them,' he said. 'Keep walking, and do whatever I tell you.'

He linked a hand around Simone's upper arm to keep full control of her, and together they walked down the promenade. They went past their hotel, then, when it was a couple of hundred yards behind them, George said: 'Now we cross the road.'

On the other side, they continued on, away from the hotel. Anderson and the other two kept abreast of them, on the promenade side of the road.

'See that bus,' George said, nodding towards one coming along the front in their direction. 'We're going to get on it if it stops for the lights.'

'What if it doesn't?'

'Then we get the next.'

Five minutes later they were a mile away in Brighton's main shopping area, their three pursuers lost somewhere behind them. They hopped the bus when George saw a taxi free, and got the driver to take them to the hotel's rear entrance.

Once inside they felt calmer, more secure.

In the lift, George said: 'We pick up Cathy, then we get back to London. Right?'

'What then?'

'For God's sake, I don't know! See what happens next.'

They rode the lift to the floor above the one with their rooms, then used the emergency staircase.

All was silent in the long corridor.

George said: 'I think we're going to make it. Have you got the key?'

Simone nodded, and rummaged in her bag.

As she opened the door, George smelt cigar smoke.

Mortwell was there, sitting in an easy chair beside the bed. He held the cigar delicately in one hand; in the other he cradled the white rabbit, Arthur, against his chest. Small grey tubes of cigar ash lay in a circle on the carpet around his feet.

He was not smiling.

Cathy was asleep on the bed, her fragile, tattooed hand tucked under her face like the paw of a slumbering kitten.

George and Simone froze at the sight of him, then Simone gasped and moved towards the girl.

Mortwell raised his hand, and she halted.

'Ssh,' he said. 'We don't want to wake her, do we?'

George started to say: 'How the – ?'

'You bloody fool, George . . . you bloody fool.'

'Can't you leave it, Dinny?'

'No . . . I don't think I can. Not going to leave it at

191

all.' He stood up, and put the rabbit down on the seat. He walked around them, and pushed the door to. 'Am I, lovey?' he said to Simone. 'Never did leave it, not going to start now.'

George looked quickly at the bed, thinking of the gun there, somewhere beneath Cathy's head.

Mortwell was pacing around, and he noticed George's look.

'Nothing there for you, Georgie,' he said. 'A little tart, shot through with horse, saving herself for this bitch.'

He rounded suddenly on Simone, and with a shocking violence smashed the flat of his hand against her face.

Simone's head was turned by the blow, but instantly she faced him again. She had started to breathe with a weird, painful rasping noise.

Mortwell took a fistful of Simone's blouse, twisted it to get a good grip, then pulled her forward.

'Look at this tart, George. What do you say?'

'Fucking leave it out, Dinny.'

Mortwell shook his head from side to side, making a tutting noise with his tongue.

'A stinking black tart, George. That's what you've been doing it for. Look at her . . . a cheap black whore.' He tightened his grip on her, pulled her face close to his. 'I'm not going to hurt you . . . your pimp does that for me.'

But he punched her again, this time with his fist. George heard the deeply unpleasant sound of bone cracking bone, and Simone appeared to slump.

Mortwell flung her to the floor, and she sprawled.

George dived across the room, shoved Cathy out of the way and grabbed for the gun.

It was not there.

Simone rolled over painfully, tried to get up. George saw a trickle of blood coming from one of her nostrils, dark against her skin. Cathy, confused and frightened, screamed shrilly.

Mortwell said: 'Now look what you –'

Simone, on her knees, had opened her bag and taken out George's Walther automatic. She raised it in both hands, aimed it at Mortwell's chest and pulled the trigger. The bullet struck him just below his throat, flinging him back against the wall. Blood streaked vivid scars on the floral wallpaper. Mortwell, leaning as if pinned to the wall, made a vile croaking noise. Then he slumped, with a noisy jerking rattle of jaw and limbs.

'It fucking hurts, doesn't it?' Simone shouted. Still on her knees she faced Mortwell again, and pumped another bullet into his body.

'*Simone!*' George screamed. 'Pack it in!'

The door banged open abruptly, and Anderson was there with the other two. He took in what had happened at a glance, then advanced rapidly on Simone. He was carrying a long-bladed knife.

'Gimme the gun, bitch!'

'It really fucking hurts!' Simone cried.

She turned the gun on him, pulled the trigger, and Anderson spun violently in mid-stride, the blood exploding from his shattered chest. He collapsed in the doorway, twitching and dying.

Dudley and Terry ran away.

Simone stood up, sweat running down from her brow, mingling with the blood. She held the gun steady, both hands firm on the stock, two fingers compressing the trigger past its safety point.

Cathy, on the bed, was sprawling face down, screeching and sobbing helplessly.

Simone took a step towards George, the barrel pointing square at his face.

'Now you,' she said.

George went cold inside, his entire universe closing down and concentrating on the slug that lay waiting for him, six inches away.

He said: 'Come on, then.'

Simone's fingers tightened, and the barrel shook minutely.

'It would hurt you too.'

'Give me the gun,' George said, and it seemed to him his voice came high and shrill, emanating from a point somewhere behind him.

'I'll do it!' she said.

'Why?'

'Because . . . Because you're *nothing*!'

'And I'm cheap.'

George's eyes flickered towards Mortwell's body, and for an instant she was distracted. The gun wavered.

George smacked her furiously around the head, then he ducked to the side. He brought the heel of his hand down hard on her wrist and the gun crashed to the floor.

Simone reeled around, and fell loosely against the side of the bed. She was shaking, but she made no sound.

George said: 'You fucking *cow*. You would have done it, wouldn't you? You bloody bitch.'

Simone turned her head to face him. Her eyes were dry and cold.

'You still don't know anything, do you?' she said.

The rabbit had hopped on to the bed, and was snuffling against Cathy's naked legs.

George stepped over Anderson's body, and went out into the corridor. People were there, a safe distance away, staring in horror at the blood spattered across the walls.

He went down to the promenade, walked along it in the sunshine, ignoring the crowds. When he came to some steps he walked down them, and came to a lower level where changing huts had been built. A girl was lying in front of one of them, sunbathing on a towel. She lay face down, her bikini top undone.

George walked past her and went to the rail. He rested his trembling hands on the warm metal and stared across the stony beach towards the sea. It was nearly midday, and the sun sparkled dazzlingly from the smooth water. George shook with nausea, and the reactions from violent exertion, anger . . . and fear.

Along the promenade above and behind him, seeming far away and remote from his life, the sound of police sirens brought discordancy to the scene. Several of them went past, but one came to a halt on the road behind him.

People on the beach below had also heard the noise, and now they were looking towards the high concrete promenade, shading their eyes, raising themselves on tiptoes to see better. The girl on the towel sat up too, tying the strings of her bikini top. She put on sunglasses, then stood up.

George turned at last. Two police officers were up by the rail of the promenade, looking down towards him. One of the women he had seen in the corridor was with them, and she was pointing at him.

Uncaring of what was going to happen to himself, George shrugged his shoulders, thrust his hands deep into the pockets of his trousers, and went slowly up the steps to meet them.

Epilogue

The prison officer opened the gate for him, and George walked into the outside world. It was a mild day, the sun just visible through a thin layer of cloud. He took a couple of deep breaths, trying to expel the stink of prisons from his lungs.

Thomas was there, waiting for him, leaning casually against the side of the Jaguar.

'You're not supposed to park outside prisons,' George said amiably.

'It doesn't matter. I haven't been here long.'

George turned to look back at the prison gate. The officer was watching him curiously, so George raised a hand to wave to her. She backed away at once, and slammed the gate behind her.

'How's it doing?' George said to Thomas.

'Not so bad. But you'll find things have changed a bit. Since you've been inside, you know.'

George gave him a quizzical look.

'I was only in there for an hour and a bleeding half!' he said.

'Aye . . . even so.'

George threw a mock punch at him, and Thomas pretended to double up.

'Where's Jeanie?' George said. He looked in through the window at the back of the car and saw her schoolbag lying on the seat.

'She didn't want to wait. You were gone too long.'

'What, walked off? Just like that?'

'I tried to make her wait, but you know . . .'

George glanced back at the bleak edifice of Holloway Prison. 'I'd like to get away from here,' he said.

'She won't be long. Said she was going to buy you something. So . . . how was three T's and a B?'

'Seemed all right to me. Settling down for a long wait . . . you know how it is.'

'No, but you do,' Thomas said.

'Yeah.' George took the ignition key from his pocket and moved into the driver's seat. Thomas slid into the seat beside him. George reached forward into the dash and found his tape. He rattled it into the slot, and in a moment the smooth melodic sound of Nat 'King' Cole came trickling out.

Thomas said: 'You still like that, then?'

'Makes me think of the old days.'

'That's what I meant.'

'Well, you know –'

'I don't, actually,' Thomas said.

George heard someone moving by the car, and he turned. Jeanie had appeared by the driver's window. She leaned through and kissed him on the cheek.

'I bought you a present, Dad.'

She passed him a small paper bag, with something plastic and oblong inside.

'What is it?' He shook it to and fro beside his ear, pretending to be suspicious.

'*Open* it. Thomas and I think you need it.'

It was a tape cassette.

'Oh . . . thanks.' Jeanie clambered into the back seat, and leaned forward with her elbows resting on the backs of their seats. 'I suppose you want me to put it on,' George said.

Thomas said: 'We had a vote while you were in there. We don't want to listen to *Mona Lisa* again. Ever.'

'What's wrong with it?'

Thomas replied by leaning forward and hitting the eject button. He took the new cassette from George, and slotted it in.

'Drive, George.'

A few moments later they heard *Here Comes the Sun*.

'Better?' said Thomas.

'All right.' In the rear-view mirror he could see Jeanie smiling at him. 'Yeah . . . it's better. Thanks, love.'

He drove down to Holloway Road, turned left and started up the long hill towards Highgate.

'I thought we were going home, Dad.'

'Not yet. It's a nice day . . . let's have a walk on Hampstead Heath.'

Jeanie settled back and looked through the window at the drab old buildings they were passing.

George said: 'They cut all her hair off.'

'Whose?'

'You know . . . three T's.'

'All of it?'

'Most of it. And she was wearing overalls. Never seen her like that before.' He stared ahead, listening to the music, thinking about Simone in a new way. 'I got it all figured out now, Thomas. I was just her driver for a while. Whatever else might have happened, the other stuff, the hotels, the look in her eye,

199

the whole damn thing . . . I was just the driver.'

'It isn't much of a story.'

'You read too many books.'

'But you liked her, George . . . you really liked her.'

'Nah.' George drove through Highgate Village, then took the side road towards the Heath. 'I didn't know her, did I?'

'Macabre, moony and plain strip-joint sleazy'
SUNDAY TIMES

SNOW WHITE
AND ROSE RED
by ED McBAIN

Sarah Whittaker, said her attorney, was nuttier than a
fruitcake. When Matthew Hope visited her in the institution he
was half-expecting some shaven-headed basket case in a
uniform that looked like mattress ticking.

Instead Sarah Whittaker was wearing a wheat-coloured linen
suit and a saffron silk blouse open at the throat. She had a
generous mouth and eyes as green as the Amazon jungle and
Matthew Hope fell in love with her on the spot.

'So why are you here?' he asked. 'Ah,' she said, and started
to tell him a story. And it certainly wasn't the kind of tale a
mother would read to her children at bedtime . . .

**'A swift and adroitly plotted mystery . . . events leave the
reader devastated'.**
PUBLISHERS WEEKLY

**'Laces its horrors with some good running gags and
some gamey writing . . . everything one looks for in
vintage McBain'.**
THE FICTION MAGAZINE

0 7221 5726 6   CRIME   £2.95

SEVEN STEPS TO TREASON

Michael Hartland

0 7221 4201 3   Adventure Thriller   £2.50

DUNN'S CONUNDRUM
STAN LEE

Harry Dunn seemed to have out-spied the masters when he set up the library. Twelve people worked there, and they had access to absolutely everything. All the strategic information, all the secrets big and small – on tape, on film and on paper, they had the lot.

But one of the Librarians had somehow beaten the system, and had clandestinely leaked their biggest secret of all. And with East–West relations reaching countdown level, that left Harry with one hell of a headache . . .

0 7221 5485 2   ADVENTURE THRILLER   £2.95

A selection of bestsellers from SPHERE

FICTION

GOLDEN TRIPLE TIME	Zoe Garrison	£2.95 ☐
BEACHES	Iris Rainer Dart	£2.95 ☐
RAINBOW SOLDIERS	Walter Winward	£3.50 ☐
FAMILY ALBUM	Danielle Steel	£2.95 ☐

FILM AND TV TIE-IN

BLOCKBUSTERS GOLD RUN		£1.95 ☐
9½ WEEKS	Elizabeth McNeil	£1.95 ☐
BOON	Anthony Masters	£2.50 ☐
AUF WIEDERSEHEN PET 2	Fred Taylor	£2.75 ☐

NON-FICTION

THE LAST NAZI: THE LIFE AND TIMES OF JOSEPH MENGELE	Gerald Astor	£3.50 ☐
THE FALL OF SAIGON	David Butler	£3.95 ☐
LET'S FACE IT	Christine Piff	£2.50 ☐
LIVING WITH DOGS	Sheila Hocken	£3.50 ☐

All Sphere books are available at your local bookshop or newsagent, or can be ordered direct from the publisher. Just tick the titles you want and fill in the form below.

Name _____

Address _____

_____

Write to Sphere Books, Cash Sales Department, P.O. Box 11, Falmouth, Cornwall TR10 9EN.

Please enclose cheque or postal order to the value of the cover price plus:

UK: 55p for the first book, 22p for the second and 14p per copy for each additional book ordered to a maximum charge of £1.75.

OVERSEAS: £1.00 for the first book and 25p for each additional book.

BFPO & EIRE: 55p for the first book, 22p for the second book plus 14p per copy for the next 7 books, thereafter 8p per book.

Sphere Books reserve the right to show new retail prices on covers which may differ from those previously advertised in the text or elsewhere, and to increase postal rates in accordance with the PO.